Their

Perfect

Christmas

Silver Fox Christmas Book 1

Katie O'Connor

Snarky Heart Press

Their Perfect Christmas

Silver Fox Christmas Book 1

Katie O'Connor

Snarky Heart Press

-Their Perfect Christmas-
-A Silver Fox Christmas Book 1-

ISBN: Kindle Edition 978-1-989816-60-8
ISBN: Print Edition 978-1-989816-59-2
ISBN: Other Digital Versions 978-1-989816-61-5

Published December 2022
(katieohwrites.com)

Cover by Laura Heritage: P.S. Cover Designs
Editing by Samantha Talarico

Dedication

To all the teachers and librarians out there.
I appreciate your hard work and dedication.

Their Perfect Christmas

Welcome to Christmas in Valley Springs the place that proves that the heart can still find love as you get older. Valley Springs is the home of the hottest silver foxes in Canada. Pop in for a while, read these heart-touching holiday romances featuring ladies and gentlemen in their fifties.

♥♥♥

Declan Foxx has a well-kept secret. Not even his family knows what he actually does for a living. Until he bumps into Cynthia Thomas, he likes it that way. She might be the woman of his dreams, as well as his biggest fan.

Cynthia Thomas loves being a librarian but she's stumped because she can't find any information about her favorite author, the reclusive DR Thomas. Little does she know he's sitting in her library working up the courage to ask her out.

With the holidays fast approaching, both Declan and Cynthia are looking for love, if they can get beyond their crippling shyness. Neither are getting any younger.

Can this silver fox break free of the chains on his heart and win the heart of the woman he's always dreamed of, or will shyness steal Their Perfect Christmas?

Chapter One

Declan Foxx wandered up and down the aisles between stacks of books in the Valley Springs Municipal Library. He wasn't looking for a book; he was looking for the head librarian, and she was nowhere to be found. Dang it.

He walked the short distance to the library three times a week and checked out books on the off chance that he'd see her. It was insane. He kept going to the library to find her and yet never managed to work up the courage to talk about anything besides books. He'd been hoping today he could muster up his courage and ask her out. Maybe it would be his lucky day.

Nope.

He paused before a seasonal display. Pumpkins, rats, skeletons, and ghosts covered a three by six-foot table. Between the knickknacks, piles of Halloween books and DVDs were displayed enticingly. She'd really outdone herself this time. Of course, all of her displays were alluring. This one was great, and nothing made him chuckle like whimsical Halloween decorations. He looked through some books, focusing on the true ghost stories rather than the gore. He loved a good shoot-em-up movie, but gore didn't move him at all. However, the possibility of ghosts intrigued his creative mind.

With a book on ghosts of Alberta in his hand, he wandered down the fiction aisles and paused in front of the space where his novels should be. Three out of five of his novels were checked out. He'd donated the books anonymously to the library and was thrilled that they were being read. He pulled one off the shelf. The pages were dog-eared; the cover curled. It had been read more than once. For a moment, he wished for the old-school checkout sleeves in the back of books so he could see how many times it had been read.

Vanity, your name is Declan Foxx.

"Have you read that?"

It was her. Library Girl, as he'd dubbed the head librarian and the woman he was mustering the courage to ask out. At fifty-two, you'd think he'd be able to ask a woman on a date. His heart thumped erratically. She was lovely. Her smile stole his breath, even when he saw her at a distance. She was average height, and probably average weight.

Her skirt was a modest length, and her pumpkin orange sweater hinted at curves he'd like to get to know. She had a few laugh lines and a bit of grey sprinkled in her red-brown hair. She wore the sexiest dark brown, almost black, large-framed glasses. She was the stereotypical sexy librarian and the loveliest woman he'd ever seen. He liked that she didn't try to hide her age. He thought she was about his age, unless he missed his guess.

Ask her out.

"Um. Yeah, I have read it." *You could say that; I wrote it.* He kept the thought to himself.

"What did you think? I adore DR Thomas's books. It's a shame he only featured the dragons in one book; I'd like to see more of them, and I wish he wrote faster." Her eyes sparkled with excitement. Was there anything hotter than a woman who loved books, especially his books?

"I expect it takes a lot of work to write a book. I've read that it can take as much as two years after a book is finished for it to get out in print. I don't know how accurate that is." His first had taken three years if you included the seven rounds of edits it had undergone. His fourth one took six months. Being popular could speed things up in the publishing game.

"Wow. I didn't know that." She laughed, and the hair on his arms rose at the light, airy sound. She was potent, just by being alive.

He shrugged. "It's what I've heard."

"I read a rumor on a library chat loop that DR Thomas has quit writing. Another one said he was dead. I sure hope both are wrong, especially the last one. I need closure on the series. I hope his new one is already at the publisher's. It's been a year since his last release, and I'm chomping at the bit for the next one." In her enthusiasm, she looked like an eager schoolgirl.

He could think of a thing or two he'd like her to chomp on. Right, as if he could even ask her out. She was too pretty, too kind, too everything. His tongue barely worked, and his mind stammered like a stuck record. He swallowed repeatedly to remove the cotton from his mouth and lump from his throat.

"Have you read them all? You really should. They're delicious. They're kind of like a space western meets adventure meets shooter movie. So good." She sighed dramatically.

He really should tell her that he was the author. It might be his in to getting a date. Heck, maybe she'd ask him out.

"Library lady? Can you help me?" A little girl about four years old stood at the end of the aisle looking hopeful.

"Certainly, Lisa. Come on. Let's get you what you need." She hurried away and turned back at the end of the row. "Talk to you later. You really should read them all!"

She was gone then, and he was standing there like a teenage boy with his first crush. He'd never managed to ask Mandy Nicholson out either. Or Shayla, or Tahira, or Ashley. After being asked to the prom by Francine Boatman and then dumped by her, he'd never manned up enough to ask another woman out.

At university, the only women he'd talked to were in his study groups and that was strictly related to assignments. No dates. No coffees. He was pathetic.

He slid the book back on the shelf, being sure to put it in the correct place. A little further along, he found a Michael Crichton book he hadn't read yet. He grabbed that and a book by Canadian author Dwayne Clayden and added them to his growing pile. Maybe this week, he'd actually write something as well as reading these books. Sure, he'd probably write a few sad words after talking to her, but then his inspiration would dry up.

It had been almost two years since he'd first seen her, and the only time he managed to write anything was after he chatted with her. She'd simultaneously stolen and become his muse.

Hoping Library Girl would be at the desk, he headed toward the exit. He really needed to find out her name. Mona, one of the other library staff members, was there, but his dream date was nowhere in sight. Dang. "Hi, Mona," he said. "How are the kids?"

"They're holy terrors. They're going to drive me to drink, I swear it." She laughed.

"You love them to bits and you know it." How come he could talk to married women and old ladies, but not pretty or single ones? Being the brunt of a prom night prank had left scars. Deep scars. He knew the experience shouldn't still matter, but it did.

"I do indeed. But they're so jacked up about Halloween, they're not sleeping. I can't wait until the Christmas season starts." She rolled her eyes and checked out his books. "You come in a lot."

"I read a lot."

"Hm. Wouldn't have anything to do with a pretty redheaded librarian, would it?"

"She's not exactly a redhead. She's sort of between strawberry blonde and mahogany. It changes colors under different light." Why did he have to say that? He might as well have admitted that Mona was right.

"You are interested then. You should ask her out. She watches you too, you know." She winked. "You'd make a cute couple."

She looked like she was going to keep talking, so he interrupted. "Can I have my books?" He looked at his old-school watch. "I've got an appointment."

"Coward." She laughed again and slid the stack across the desk. "See you in a couple days. She's on holidays next week."

"Thanks… Take care of those kids. Tell Andre I said hi. Maybe he and I can go play darts at the pub one night next week."

"I'll tell him to call you."

He hurried out of the library as fast as his legs would move. Crap. He didn't want anyone to know that he was interested in Library Girl. Dang. He had been too embarrassed to ask Mona her name. Another missed chance. They were piling up, and he wasn't getting any younger. Worse, the more he missed opportunities to ask her out, the deeper he sank into writer's block. His social ineptitude was killing his inspiration.

Today was the closest he'd been to her in weeks. Still, he'd messed it up. It was going to take a miracle to go on a date with her. Well, Halloween was the time of miracles. No, wait; that was Christmas. He'd better work up the courage to ask her out before Christmas if he wanted a Christmas miracle of his own. Maybe Santa would bring him a librarian for Christmas.

Trying not to drag his feet, he headed for his truck.

Filled with sudden resolve, he turned and went back inside.

"You just missed her. She skipped out the back for lunch."

"Dammit."

"No cussing in the library," Mona teased. "You might catch her at Barb's Café."

He was out the door and back in the parking lot in seconds. He threw the books in his truck, wincing as they bounced off the seat onto the floor. He'd replace them if they were damaged. He could afford it. Right now, he had to find Library Girl before she vanished along with his courage.

He raced toward the café and slammed through the door. It was empty. He tried every eating establishment on Main Street without luck. Too little, too late.

Despondent, he returned to his vehicle and went home to stare at the laptop that haunted him.

Cynthia Jones hurried from the library. The second he was gone, she'd bolted, claiming she couldn't wait any longer for lunch. She had to get outside and cool off. A stiff fall breeze blew the heat from her cheeks as she marched down the street, away from Valley Springs's main road and shopping area.

Why couldn't she work up the courage to ask him out?

She'd never considered herself shy, just a bit reserved, and not particularly outgoing, except with library patrons. Usually, she could talk to anyone. She'd asked men out before. Not recently. But when she was younger, she had known no fear. That was before she was married. After her marriage turned loveless and she was divorced, she'd just sort of stopping going out.

She hadn't been attracted to a man in years. Honestly, at her age, her libido wasn't what it once was. Sure, she had urges. Plenty of them. But few men had tickled her fancy since she'd fallen in love with the mysterious author DR Thomas.

"You don't even know where he lives, or what he looks like. You're an idiot." She sighed at her self-disgust. She wasn't an idiot. She was an intelligent woman with a fabulous career. She looked good for her age; regular visits to the gym kept her fit. She would be a great catch for some guy. Instead, she was hooked on an author without a picture who had a totally lame bio on his book jackets. She didn't know how old he was. Hell, he could be twenty, or eighty, or anything in between. He might even be a she. It was ridiculous that a random author had totally seduced her heart with his words.

It wasn't until Declan Foxx arrived in the library that she thought there might be a chance with another man. If she could work up the courage to ask him out, because clearly, he wasn't going to ask her.

Declan Foxx. Even his name was masculine. She'd committed it to memory the first time she'd checked out his books. He was in a lot and always taking out two or three books. Sometimes fiction, sometime nonfiction. He was a reader, and that was damned sexy in a man. Never mind that he smelled amazing, like trees and sunshine. If he had hot reading glasses, she'd be a puddle of goo on the carpet.

She kept walking until she got to Dan's Donuts. She needed a sugar fix. Dan and his wife Suzanne had the best donuts in a five-hundred-mile radius.

"Morning, Cyn," Dan greeted her. "You're early this week, you usually don't come in until Saturday."

"I need a sugar fix. I'll take two maple-bacon donuts, a cheese croissant, an iced tea, and a dozen pumpkin tarts, please." She inhaled the heady smell of yeast. Oh, was that minced meat and pumpkin pie? Her stomach growled.

"That's a sugar fix for sure. We've got a great ham and Swiss on a cheese croissant, if you want some real food," Suzanne put in from beside the cash register.

"You know what? That sounds delicious. I'll take that instead of a plain croissant, and I'll eat it here, and the donuts, but I'll take the tarts back to work with me. I kind of abandoned everyone in my sudden quest for sugar."

"Ah, the apology sweets." Dan laughed. "We do big business in those." He bustled around prepping her order. "You going to the Winterfest dance this year?"

"Probably not. I'm not much for social events. Besides, I hear it's nearly sold out. They should raise some good funds for the hospital."

"They will; Christmas brings out the generosity in people. If you want to come, we have a couple spare tickets. Just let me know and I'll bring them by the library," Dan said.

"And I've got a couple of costumes that will fit you perfectly," Suzanne added. The annual event was Christmas party meets costume ball and always a huge hit. She went almost every year.

"Thanks." She took her lunch and sat at a table by the window. She could join her roommates at the dance again and probably end up standing at the side watching the dancers float by. Kids these days might dance alone, or in groups, but she was older; at fifty-three, she didn't want to make a spectacle of herself by dancing alone. But she'd love to slow dance with Declan.

She couldn't think of anyone to ask to the dance, except Declan, and she could barely talk to him. Plus, he hardly noticed her. Maybe she'd just stay home, curled up with a good book and a cup of tea. She could search the internet for a picture of the never photographed DR Thomas. She'd already searched a hundred times, but new stuff appeared on the web every day. She might get lucky.

Lucky. She'd like to get lucky with Declan. He had those incredible brown eyes and that strong fit body. His dark hair was sprinkled with grey. She guessed him to be about her age and that made him even more enticing. Yes, she'd love to get closer to Declan.

Great, now she was delusional as well as being a coward. When had her life turned to crap? Probably the day her childhood sweetheart and husband dumped her for a much younger woman. That's when she'd thrown herself into her career and quickly scaled the ladder in the Edmonton Public Library. When she'd stalled there, she'd followed her friends Nora and Eve to Valley Springs and a new job as head librarian.

She really had it all. Good friends, a great job, a happy home. She was healthy. Life was good, except that she couldn't really talk to Declan.

He was cute and handsome and quite well built. He smelled incredible. He was several inches taller than her five foot eight, and he was well muscled too. Maybe from working on cars all the time. He was frequently outside tinkering with someone's vehicle when she walked home from the library. She often wondered why he didn't work inside his triple garage; however, she was glad he didn't because she lived for those occasional glimpses of him, and the potential for conversation.

She shoved aside the impossible fantasy of talking to him about something significant and finished her lunch. Back at the library, she went into stalker mode and checked his account to see what he'd taken out. She was a sad excuse for a confident, successful woman.

Chapter Two

It had been over a month since Declan caught sight of Library Girl. He hadn't written a single word since then. Every Monday morning, his editor called him for an update on the progress of his much overdue book.

He should be at his computer. Instead, he was being battered by some kiddy pop hit as he entered the hardware store. The air was heavy with the smell of fresh lumber and of the potted pines lining the end of every aisle. It was like the store had a split personality. One side eagerly clearing out Halloween, the other was skating ahead to Christmas. Declan inhaled deeply as he followed his brother Tom through the store.

There were three of them in the family, all adopted. Thomas was the youngest at fifty. Ross was the oldest at fifty-four. Declan landed smack dab in the middle at fifty-two. None of them were currently married. He never had been, but both of his brothers had. Tom's ex was living in a commune style marriage where she was surrounded by the kids he couldn't give her. Ross's wife had passed away shortly after their twin sons were born, thirty-four years ago.

All in all, they were content, but he was eager to find a life mate. He just hadn't worked up the courage yet. He pushed away the discouraging thought and spoke to Tom. "Why are we here again? Don't you usually order your wood and have it delivered to the house?" Declan asked.

"Yes, but I need something special for this project. It needs to have just the right grain pattern to bring out my idea." Tom was a former high school shop teacher. He'd retired early to pursue his woodworking passion. He created works of art from wood. Furniture, sculptures, toys, whatever the wood told him to create from it.

"What are you making?" Declan pestered. He'd been bored at home and had come along on a lark. He should have stayed home and worked on his book. The one his brain wouldn't let him write. For the first time in his life, he had writer's block, and the story wouldn't come to him. No matter how many hours he sat and stared at his computer monitor, the words stayed away. Hell, he didn't even have a simple plot idea yet, just a couple thousand words of drivel that he'd probably delete later on. Tom's offer of pizza after shopping had tempted him out of the house and away from the accusations of a blank monitor.

"I'm making a desk. The top is cherry with walnut inlays. I want something different for the legs. I need to hand pick the wood. I can't risk ordering it and hoping I get what I want. If I can't find it here, I'll need to hit the city where there's better selection."

"Cool." Totally not cool. Boring was more accurate, but he was here and had to make the best of it. "I'm going to wander around. Maybe I can find a new desk lamp. Text me when you strike wood-gold."

"K." Tom was pulling slabs of wood from stacks and shoving them back in as if the conversation were over.

Dec didn't need a lamp, but it was something to do while he waited. If they weren't going for pizza later, he wouldn't have come at all. He skipped the paint aisle and a few others. He scanned the leftover Halloween decorations for a deal and spent ten minutes admiring the Christmas ornament display the staff was erecting. There was a cute typewriter ornament, and several featuring books and fireplaces. He'd have to think about a tree soon.

Eventually, he found himself standing in the lighting section, staring at a massive array of desk lamps. The one with the teddy bear base was out for sure; as were the halogen ones. He wanted something that would take an energy efficient LED bulb and not be blinding if he worked at night. His current one took a florescent and it had the slightest hum that made it hard to concentrate. He'd been living with it, but now that he was here, he'd see what his options were.

Footsteps came toward him, and he looked up, expecting to see a staff member. He couldn't contain his grin when Library Girl headed toward him. Dang, she was hot in those blue jeans and snowman print sweater. She pushed her glasses up on her nose and walked to his side. She smelled of mint and raspberries. Delicious.

"Hi," he said. *Great start.* He nearly rolled his eyes at himself. "Nice to see you." *Better.*

"Nice to see you too. Looking at lamps?" Her smile stole his breath. She was so lovely.

"Yup." He swallowed. "For my desk."

"Maybe the unicorn?" She pointed at a glittery pink unicorn lamp and smirked.

"I was thinking the brass one." It reminded him of some of the lighter shades in her hair. She was lovely, even under florescent light. The tune on the store radio morphed into Billy Joel's *Just the Way You Are*. How appropriate was that?

"I like the brass. Aren't you a mechanic? I've seen you working on cars."

He didn't know if it was the abrupt change in conversation, or her simple presence, but something had him reeling.

"I used to be a mechanic. Now I just work on cars for fun. I spend more time on the computer now and want a better lamp." He should tell her who he was, but he'd been hiding it for so long, he didn't know how to broach the subject. "I like that the brass takes LED bulbs." He couldn't even come up with something interesting to say.

"That's a great feature. I try and save energy where I can. It's why I walk to and from work, well, that and I need the exercise."

He didn't need to look at her body to know it was perfect. He stole peeks every time he was around her. If he were an artist, he could draw her from memory. She was flawless. Pretty, smart, kind, helpful, concerned about the planet. She really had it all; and he wanted it. *Er, her. He wanted her. He wanted to get to know her.* Even in his head, he was incoherent when she was close.

"You ready, girl?" a petite blonde woman called from the end of the aisle. She waved a package. "I've got my stuff."

"That's me. See you around." She was gone before he could respond.

"Who was that?" Tom's voice came from behind him.

"What?" A single word question to delay his brother until he got his brain back to normal function. "Oh, her? She works at the library. We were just discussing lamps."

"She's pretty, but probably too young for you."

"Right. I'm not that old."

"Older than me," Tom jabbed verbally, obviously trying to start a round of their teasing and bickering. One thing about his brothers, adopted though they were, they all shared the mindset that no teasing opportunity would ever slip by unused.

"At least I don't have to buy my wood," Declan shot back.

"That's low, Dec. Very low."

"Hitting below the belt?" He laughed at the pique on Tom's face. "Pizza time? I'm starved." He wasn't actually. He'd lost his appetite in the face of his inability to chase her down and ask her out, or at least get her name.

"You getting a lamp or what?"

He thought about it for a few seconds and picked up the box. "I guess I am." The lamp would look good on his desk, and he'd donate the old one to the local charity thrift shop. Besides, she'd helped him choose it.

"The library, you say?" Tom said as they walked to the front of the store.

"Yeah, why?" His brother better not get any ideas.

"Maybe I should start going to the library…" he trailed off without completing the threat.

"Do it and die," Dec growled. "Once I have my chance, if I fail, you can try. But for now, she's mine. Capisce?" No way was he letting his good-looking brother near Library Girl until he'd exhausted every chance to get to know her better.

Tom raised his arms in a surrender gesture. "Yeah, I understand. Out of respect for you, and from pity because you can't talk to women, I'll give you until the end of the year, then she's free game. You're going to have to move fast before someone else snaps her up. Like me."

"Deal." They shook hands. He was going to have to get his act together. Maybe he needed a book on overcoming shyness. He could check it out while she was working the desk. No, then she'd know how pathetic he was. He was trying to impress her, not scare her away.

Chapter Three

Cynthia dodged unpacked boxes of Halloween and Christmas décor and other shoppers as she followed Eve and Nora through the hardware store, silently fuming about being interrupted. She'd been ready to ask him out for coffee. Even the upbeat music on the intercom system didn't sooth her. Finally, she had to say something to her friends.

"Guys?" She stopped and waited for them to turn around.

"What?" they said in unison, their eyes alive with questions. People swarmed around them, hurrying on their way to someplace important.

She inhaled deeply and braced herself. "That guy, the one I was talking to back there. I like him. Well, I think I like him. He's nice, he's handsome." She pursed her lips and grimaced. "I was trying to work up the courage to ask him out when you interrupted. Could you please, please, forget you know me if you ever see me talking to him?"

"Just ask him out already," Eve said in her typical calm manner. She threw her arm around Cyn's shoulders. "I'm sure he doesn't bite."

"Or maybe he does," Nora said and made a cat's *mrow* sound and curled her hands like claws.

Cyn couldn't help but laugh. "Maybe, but I need time to find out." She needed time and courage. Why was trying to get a date so hard?

"You could have said something earlier. Why don't you go back and talk to him? We'll wait in the car, or meet you at home."

"Give me ten minutes. Meet you at the car." Suddenly fueled with enthusiasm and bravery, she rushed back to the lighting section. It was empty except for one twenty-something girl looking at table lamps. She approached the woman.

"Excuse me, did you see a dark-haired man about my age in here?"

"No, ma'am. I didn't see anyone. Good luck finding him." She smiled warmly.

"Thanks." Disappointed, she walked up and down the aisles of the store. She walked back and forth four times before giving up. She'd missed him, along with her chance to ask him out. Despondent, she wandered out to the car where her friends waited.

"Hey, girl," Nora said as Cynthia climbed into the back seat. "We're going for subs, want to come?"

"Why don't you drop me off first? I'm tired." Not tired, but a bit upset that she'd missed another chance to ask Declan out. "I think I'll read and have some tea. I've got a book to review for work."

"You do know that you don't have to read every book that comes into the library, right?" Nora put her Honda Accord into drive and pulled out of the parking lot.

"I know, but I feel it's my responsibility to be up to date on our products. It makes me a better librarian." Plus, she loved reading anything in any genre.

"It makes you a total book nerd, but we love you anyway." Eve grinned at her over the seat. "Tell us about this guy."

"Yeah, tell us," Nora echoed.

"His name is Declan. He comes into the library a lot. He reads all kinds of things. He's even read my favorite series by DR Thomas; the one you guys won't read. He's attractive and well built. He's my age, more or less, and he seems really shy. I don't think he'll ever ask me out, so I have to do it. It's hard. I'm not shy, but I'm also not used to being the aggressor in a relationship." She sighed and flopped her head back against the seat. "I'm useless."

"Not useless at all. You're a fabulous friend, a great librarian, and a wonderful adopted aunt to my daughter," Nora declared. "You just need to believe in yourself more. You need to realize that you can be open with people. You don't need to hide yourself away."

"Be brave, my friend," Eve encouraged.

"I know, it's just so hard for me." She wasn't like this in college or in the early years of her marriage. She wasn't exactly outgoing, but she wasn't so reticent either. Her jerk of an ex had surprised her when he'd dumped her. Sure, they'd being going through a rough patch. Both of them were trying to climb the ladder in their careers. The breakup had been a blow to her self-esteem still had her reeling five years later. How do you get over a betrayal like that?

"That's it," she declared. "Time to grow some balls and man up. I'm going to do this. I'm going to be brave. I can do this. No, I will do this. I will ask him out." She said the words, hoping they'd manifest into reality, but deep inside, she doubted her ability to get past herself.

"The Winterfest dance is coming up. Ask him to that." Nora pulled up in front of the two-story house they shared.

"If I see him before then, I will." She tried to sound firm but was certain her voice trembled.

"Can't you look him up in the library records and call him?" Eve suggested.

"I can't do that. Those records are confidential. I could lose my job." How could they even suggest such a thing? Though, honestly, the idea was tempting.

"Make up some library business. Get him to come in and then pounce on him." Nora and Eve laughed.

♥♥♥

Several days later, she was busy setting up her first Christmas display when Maxine from the post office rushed in.

"Oh, I have something exciting to tell you," Maxine gushed.

She didn't really want to listen to gossip, but Maxine would tell her anyway. "Oh? What's that?"

"I just discovered that we might have another author in Valley Springs. Maybe you could get him to do a talk at the library. I adore adding signed books to my collection."

"That could be fun for my patrons."

"Anyway," Maxine grabbed her arm and leaned in close, "I saw that Declan Foxx got a thick package from a publisher. He could be a writer."

"Or he could have sent them a letter about one of their authors, or something else."

"Well, I think he could be an author. You should ask him. Or at least research him on the internet and see what you find."

Later, she sat at her computer, doing just that. Nothing important came up. Certainly nothing to indicate that Declan Foxx might be an author. In truth, it was like he didn't exist at all. But not all authors were eager to have their lives publicized.

Wouldn't it be dreamy if Declan was DR Thomas? What if her hot patron was actually her favorite author? The more she thought about it, the more certain she became that Declan Foxx was indeed DR Thomas. The D in DR could stand for Declan, right?

Chapter Four

Declan checked his watch. It was almost five. He could get some work done on his truck before Library Girl walked by on her way home from work. He'd been staring at his computer all day. He hadn't even bothered to get dressed this morning. He'd better get cleaned up and get outside. He showered, grabbed a couple granola bars, and headed to the garage.

Declan glared at the sky. Light snow drifted down dusting everything sparkling white in the late afternoon light. If this kept up, he would have to quit working outside and pull the truck into the garage. He really didn't want to do that.

He was banging away trying to remove his radiator when his brother showed up.

"Ross," Dec picked up the discussion they'd abandoned on his last visit to Valley Springs, "Good to have you home. I don't know why you stay in the city." He gave Ross a one-armed man-hug, being careful not to soil his suit. Who wore a suit every day? "Life's so much easier and chill here."

"Dude, I'm fifty-four years old. It's not too late for me to find a woman. It's hard to find someone as nice as Martha. I'll never get past her death, but I know there's someone out there for me. And frankly, the ratio of single women to bachelors is higher in the city." He raked his hand through his dark brown hair.

"You better hurry up, before all those gray hairs trick women into thinking you're a senior citizen." He laughed at Ross's annoyed scowl. "Pass me that 9/16th wrench." Ross picked up the wrench with two fingers and passed it over. Dec loosened the nut on his truck's radiator. "Come live with Tom and me."

"Yeah, exactly how much call does this two-bit town have for a mathematician? I work with numbers and scientists. How many people in this town need a numbers genius?" He wasn't exaggerating, Ross was top rated in his field.

Declan bit back a smart response. No sense poking the bear and ending all possibility of his oldest brother ever leaving his high-priced, high-stress career. It was ridiculous how much he was paid. The man worked for NASA for Pete's sake. Declan wondered what had brought Ross back so soon. Last visit, he couldn't wait to leave. It was unusual for Ross to have two visits to town so close together. Usually, they landed months apart.

"I'm just saying it would be nice to have you here. Tom moved here. He's gone from teacher to carpenter and frankly, Tom's loving the transition."

"Did I hear my name?" Tom wandered across the driveway, heavy work boots thumping with each measured step. He leaned against the Dodge's bumper, bits of sawdust clung to his hair and jacket. "Yo, Ross, good to see you. You didn't stay away long. Only a week." He offered his hand. Tom never was one for displays of affection. He felt all the emotions, he just didn't show them much. "How's life in the big city? You found a woman yet?"

"Not yet, but I'm looking. How about you two? How's dating life in Valley Springs?"

The sarcasm in his voice was annoying. "Actually," Declan declared, "I've got my eye on a redhead. A very hot redhead."

"She'll need to be hot; it's freezing out here," Ross complained. "Why are you working outside when you have a perfectly good heated garage?" He stuffed his hands in his jacket pockets and hunched his shoulders against the cold.

"Because my redhead walks by every day at exactly five-fifteen on her way home from the library."

Tom laughed. "Still chasing your mythical sexy librarian?" Ross chuckled along with Tom.

"Tom, you saw her at the hardware store, admit it, she's cute."

"She's passable."

Ross laughed. He was in for a big surprise because his librarian was just about the sexiest woman Declan had ever laid eyes on. Her image flashed before his mind, as real as if she were standing there. She was about five-eight, perfect for his six-foot frame. She was slender and fit, and she wore those damn sexy oversized glassed with the dark frames. She stole his breath and tied his tongue. Sooner or later, he'd muster up the courage to start an actual conversation with his future wife.

"Just wait, you'll see how hot she is. And forget about taking a shot at her. I'm calling dibs. I saw her first, and that makes her mine."

"Dibs?" Ross laughed. "What are we, in grade school?"

"If she is hot, she's probably too young for you." Tom laughed. "What are you, sixty?"

"Funny, very funny," Declan drawled. "You know darn well I'm fifty-two."

"Like I said, she's too young for you."

Declan ignored the taunt. If he reacted, they'd just up the ante and go even further. At fourteen, he'd gotten glasses and braces, and their taunting was unbearable. After months of teasing, he'd finally learned to ignore them, and they finally gave up and found a new target.

"Hold this." He passed the wrench to Tom. It was greasy and Ross wouldn't want to risk getting grease on his Armani suit. Why a mathematician wore Armani he didn't understand, but whatever floats your boat. He grasped the top of the radiator and wiggled it upward until it was free.

"Holy hot cross buns. Would you look at that." Declan didn't need to look up to know Ross had just spotted his sexy librarian. "Sweet holy mother of God. I'd fight a tiger for a piece of that," Ross declared.

"Back off, bro."

"Not the redhead." Ross grabbed Declan by the shoulder and spun him around. The radiator thumped back into place. "Her!" He pointed. "The blonde."

Declan knocked his brother's hand down. "Dude, don't point. Didn't Mom teach you anything?" His words trailed off as he stared at the trio of woman ambling towards them in a bright wave of laughter that rippled down his arms making his hair stand up. His librarian walked between a petite brunette and a curvy blonde. "Three women, three heights, three body types," he whispered.

"Like God took everything perfectly female and divided it up to make three pieces of heaven on earth." Ross sighed.

Bundled in short dress jackets and scarves, they looked like models just off the ski hill.

"Maybe I should move home," Ross declared.

"You never mentioned that she had friends," Tom drawled, accusation heavy in his voice. "You can't have them all; that's not fair. You've been ogling her for months and not once did you mention she had friends."

"Of course, she has friends, I've just never seen more than a glimpse of them before today." Objectively speaking, her friends were as beautiful as she was, but neither took his breath away the way Library Girl did. He should have asked her name at the library or the hardware store. Something about her just drained the brain right out of his head.

He huffed out a breath. It was high school all over again. And trade school too. Too damn shy to talk to a beautiful woman. Kids, teens, grandmas, moms with kids, no problem. But a lovely potentially single woman, and his mouth filled with cotton and turned Sahara dry.

He'd long ago given up on having a family of his own. He wasn't getting any younger, but he wasn't about to give up on finding someone to love. Library Girl was probably a bit younger than he was, not a lot, but a bit. He'd been watching her, carefully checking her left hand for a ring.

She had two thumb rings and two pinkie rings, but the rest of her delicate fingers were reassuringly bare.

"Hey, isn't that Eve Farstaad?" Tom asked. "She was all the rage in galleries last year."

"Don't be crazy. Why would someone that famous be in a place like this?" Ross asked. "Famous artists don't live in tiny hick towns; they live in big cities near art galleries and museums."

Declan rolled his eyes. "Dude, you are so biased. I know at least four well-known creative people who live here, including me."

"You? Ya, you're so creative, you fix cars in your garage." Ross laughed.

"World's Most Creative Wrench Puller." Tom's baritone laugh joined Ross's.

"Excuse me?"

Dec turned toward the women who had stopped at the end of the driveway. He swallowed hard before speaking. "Hi," was all he managed to squeeze past his cotton mouth.

Library Girl spoke, "I don't mean to be rude, but aren't you DR Thomas? The sci-fi writer?" Her smile was breathtaking.

"My name is Thomas, but I'm a carpenter, not an author," Tom said.

"Not you. Him." She pointed at Declan.

His brothers laughed. "Declan write a book? He can hardly write his own name." Ross laughed louder.

Frustration rose in Declan's chest. He had to remind himself that his brother was joking. The Foxx family never passed up an opportunity to rib one another about anything. That teasing was balanced by unwavering love and support…once the teasing stopped. He loved his family, but sometime they were embarrassing.

"How did you know it was me?" He was tickled that Library Girl had figured out who he was when his own family had no idea. "There are no publicity photos of me. I've tried to maintain my anonymity. You never mentioned it before."

She hurried to his side, and he was struck by how lovely she looked with snowflakes decorating her precise hair bun.

"You are a hard man to find," she declared, placing a hand on his arm, making his heart stutter. "My girlfriend was coming here to visit this past summer. Her publisher told her DR Thomas lived here. I guess you have the same publisher. She wouldn't tell me who you were, I don't think she knew, but I've been trying to ferret it out. I'm a huge fan; you have to sign my books. Please."

Heat filled his face, and he glanced away. When he looked back, her green eyes were filled with concern.

"Oh no. I didn't mean to out you. I spent four years trying to find you. I've never read an author I adore more than you. I just wanted to get my books signed. I am so sorry."

He shrugged. "It's okay. What gave me away? Knowing DR Thomas lived in town shouldn't have been enough to tip you off."

"Yesterday, Maxine, from the post office, mentioned that you got a package from a publishing house. I don't think she meant to reveal a secret, and I know she didn't mean any harm. She's an avid reader and was excited that our very own hometown had a published author. I managed to put two and two together. Valley Springs is only twenty-eight hundred people. What are the odds that we would have a famous writer here?" She almost glittered with her excitement.

"Oh." *Crappy answer, Dec.* He was at a loss about what to say. Library Girl was talking to him, he could hardly think let alone form any sort of coherent thought. Plus, he still didn't know her name. He should ask since he'd failed to do so a hundred times before now.

"How come your friends don't know?" She looked chagrinned at outing him.

"Brothers, not friends. Those two knuckleheads are my brothers." Ross and Tom had moved away and were talking animatedly with Library Girl's friends. "We're all adopted. That's why we don't look alike. Ross, he's the one with the black hair—well, except the grey by his ears—he's the oldest. Tom, the blonde, is the baby." He paused. "You already know I'm Declan, but everyone calls me Dec. Like deck, but without the K." He wanted to groan at the stupid explanation.

Her eyes lit up. "Declan. That's the D in DR Thomas. R for Ross. And Thomas for your author surname. You used your family's names, that is so cool." She slapped a hand over her mouth, her eyes went wide. She lowered her hand and stuffed it into her pocket. "I'm so rude. Where are my manners? I'm Cynthia Jones. Call me Cyn. Well, except in the library; there, I'm Ms. Jones to the kids, which sounds like somebody's dowager aunt." A light laugh followed her comment. It was like tiny bells, bright and delicate.

"Nice to meet you, Cynthia. Cyn." He looked at his hand. "I'd offer to shake your hand, but I'm filthy."

"No worries. Nice to meet you. It's cool that you write books and fix cars. But we should go, I guess. I should let you get back to work. Will you sign my books sometime?"

Her blush was adorable. "Yeah, I guess." Being asked for an autograph was weird. It didn't even feel flattering, just awkward. "I can come by the library…if you want."

He'd rather do it in private, but didn't want to risk seeming creepy. "Which is your favorite story?" He wasn't much for talking about himself or his books, his inner introvert didn't like it, which was part of why he'd taken a pen name. Anonymity was good, but he'd do anything to prolong this conversation. It had been way too long in coming.

"Oh, number three for sure. *Firefall* was incredible. The dragons are the best. I was disappointed they didn't play a bigger role in books four and five. You've got to bring them back in to book six. Oh, or write an entire dragon series." Her wide smile turned to a frown. "Oh, but that's probably more fantasy than true sci-fi." The funny thing was, he missed the dragons he'd created and was considering pulling them back into the current book, to see if his muse kicked back in.

"Aren't mixed-genre novels a thing now?"

Her friends had wandered away from their own conversations with his brothers before she could answer.

"Hey, Cyn," Eve said. "We'd better go."

She turned to face her friends. "Oh, right. I guess." She looked back at Dec. "I'd love to talk writing with you sometime. Come by the library. Ask for me. Please."

"I'll do that." His insides quivered. Either from excitement or trepidation, he wasn't sure which. He wanted to shout to the heavens. He'd learned Library Girl's name. Cynthia. It suited her.

Chapter Five

Once they were out of earshot of Declan, Cynthia growled at her friend, "What the heck? I was talking to Declan, and he's so hot. Didn't we just have this discussion? I can't believe my hot patron from the library is actually is DR Thomas." She fanned her face. "Why did you interrupt us?"

"I've got a commission to finish," Eve said. "I need to get it done today because I'm meeting Tom for drinks tomorrow night." She grinned. She giggled until her shoulders shook and her brunette hair waved wildly.

"Really?" Nora said. "I'm meeting Ross for drinks tomorrow too. Crazy."

"Well, aren't you lucky." She couldn't stop the pout from showing in her voice. Declan hadn't asked her out. Of course, for all she knew, her friends had done the asking. Both were much more outgoing that she was.

"Where are you meeting?" Eve asked.

"The Ram's Head Pub."

"Hey, us too. At seven-thirty."

"Yup. We could totally get them to invite their brother and Cyn could join us."

"No way! I don't want a pity date. You guys go. I'll stay home." Like the lonely old spinster that she was. They lived together in Nora's four-bedroom house on Ranch Road, right at the edge of town. Nora's ex and her daughter, Melissa, lived next door, except on the days that Nora had custody of the thirteen-year-old.

"You totally should let us. We haven't been on a group date since college," Eve decreed. "You'll have a blast."

"Right. Like I'd have fun being tongue tied around my absolute favorite author. I'd probably do something totally stupid and go all fangirl on him. I'm already so embarrassed that I blurted out his pen name. His brothers had no idea. I don't think they believed me." She was completely mortified. She wasn't some blushing teenager faced with a pop idol. She was a fifty-three-year-old woman. Mature. Confident. Smart. And she'd totally gushed all over him. She almost wished she'd never met him. Now all her secret fantasies of meeting the mysterious DR Thomas and doing unspeakable things with him were dashed. Life sucked.

Of course, learning that the handsome Declan was also her book-crush was amazing. She hugged herself, pretending it was him. But she didn't understand why he didn't say something after she'd raved over his books.

"Hey, going to the pub with us will be fun," Nora laughed.

Cyn couldn't ask for better friends than Nora and Eve. They'd met on campus and had become friends. Gosh, that was so long ago. They'd stuck together through thick and thin. Nora's wedding, marriage, and divorce. Eve's cancer and recovery. Eve having her dick of an ex dump her during chemo. They'd been through a lot.

The three of them shouldn't mesh so well. Eve, a very petite brunette with golden brown eyes, was very chill. She lived for her metal sculptures and yoga classes. Nora called herself a hot mess and not just because she spent half her life covered in paint with her blonde hair yanked back in a messy bun or covered by a paint-splattered scarf. Cynthia was the odd woman out. Her friends always teased her for being the intellectual in the group, always with her nose buried in a book, and uncomfortable in many social situations.

At the library, it was different. She was surrounded by her best friends, books. She was in charge there, and it gave her the confidence she lacked in real life. She'd never have been so brazen as to approach DR Thomas publicly if they'd met at the library. She'd have been much more discrete. She'd made such a fool of herself. But yesterday, when she'd put Maxine's information together with DR Thomas's name and come up with Declan, she'd been floored. She'd been talking to her favorite author for two years and hadn't even known it.

"It would not be fun. You'd be on dates, and I'd be sitting, trying not to say something stupid to my favorite author of all time." She waved dismissively. "Thanks, but no thanks."

As they headed toward home, the breeze blew snow in her face. It wasn't too cold outside. Without the wind, it would be the perfect day for a long walk. Right now, the wind was cutting right through her stockings and freezing her legs. Even with knee-high winter dress boots and a knee-length skirt, she was cold. Her glasses were fogging up. "Step up the pace, before I freeze solid."

"You just want to cuddle up with a DR Thomas book and fantasize about the author." Eve laughed. "Because even I have to admit that Declan was hot."

"Declan, no way," Nora argued. "Ross was totally drool worthy." She stopped mid-step. "What are the odds that three best friends would meet three totally hot bachelor brothers? And just for your information, they are all single; I asked."

"It defies math. The universe is sending us a dream," Eve declared with unusual excitement. "I'm so glad Nora convinced us all to move here."

"I was lucky the head librarian position opened up. I don't know how I'd make a living here without the library." Cyn smiled. She adored her job. She'd worked her way up from general staff in the Edmonton Public Library. She'd risen higher and higher over the years but had never managed becoming the head of a single branch, let alone of the entire system.

Valley Springs might be a small town, but if she stayed within her library budget, she had total control over what was brought in. She'd even created a special section for books that had been banned in other places. She'd had to fight town council on that a bit, but in the end, she'd won. It had taken four years to accrue the collection, and she'd purchased several of the books with her own money. After all, her rent was cheap, she didn't travel, she'd built up more than enough money to retire on, what else did she have to spend money on?

"Come on, I'm freezing. We can discuss this over dinner because I'm also starving." They scurried down the street, took a left, and after six more blocks, they were home. Usually, she loved the three-mile walk to and from work, but it was the start of winter, and as usual, she was having trouble adapting to the cooler weather. It was probably time to start dressing more warmly, but she wasn't ready to waddle to work in a snowsuit yet; however, she knew those days were coming.

Once inside, she changed out of her professional clothing, eagerly slipping into yoga pants and a slouchy sweatshirt. She turned on the kettle and pulled ingredients for spinach salad from the fridge. Eve was making some kind of pasta dish, though she wouldn't reveal exactly what it was. It involved chicken and marinara sauce, two of Cyn's favorite foods. Nora was whipping up beet greens and cream cheese sauce.

They ate quickly, without lingering because both of her friends had work to do. Eve had her commission, and Nora had a sudden inspiration and took off for her paint studio over their attached garage. In almost no time, Cyn sat at the table alone, staring at the dirty dishes. She smiled to herself. She adored her roommates. Friends since university, they were all unique and blended well together. They lived in harmony, despite their different temperaments.

Rather than run the dishwasher, she filled the sink and started washing up, a soft smile played on her lips. She'd actually met DR Thomas. And he'd been gorgeous. With his sparkling brown eyes and his dark hair with strands of grey intermingled, he was breathtaking.

His biographies always just said he lived in small-town Canada with his cat. They never mentioned an age. Somehow, in her mind, he'd been either much younger or older. Instead, he seemed close to her own age of fifty-three. And he was Declan! Her favorite library client and the stuff of fantasies.

She was rather titillated that she'd met him and he hadn't condemned her for outing his identity to his family. How could you be a famous author and not tell everyone? She'd be blurting it all over. Book signings, TV appearances. There were rumors of a major studio wanting to make a movie from book one in his series. How could he keep that to himself? She was a very private person, but some things were meant to share.

Hands deep in soapy water, she did a happy dance. She'd actually met him. Her idol, her favorite author. He'd been nice and kind. And she would get to meet him again. He'd sign her books. All of them. She had every one of his books in hardback, paperback, audiobook, and on her e-reader. She was a total DR Thomas addict. His books were her favorite go-to books. Occasionally, her addiction to his words kept her from reading what she should be evaluating for the library. She liked to read as much fiction as she could so she could speak knowledgeably when patrons asked her questions.

How great was it that her reading habit helped her do her job better?

Dishes done, she made herself a cup of lavender-chamomile tea and flipped out the lights. With her roommates in the creative zone, she wouldn't see any more of them tonight and maybe not tomorrow. Mixed blessing. She'd miss them, but she'd be able to read uninterrupted for the entire evening. She climbed the stairs to her room and set her tea on the bedside table.

While her bed was a pain to make, it was the perfect reading nook. She'd placed it in the corner so she could prop herself on a pile of pillows and read. With the pillows stacked at the intersection of two walls, they didn't slide sideways when she snuggled in to read. She adjusted the pillows and slipped into her warmest jammies. She opened her drapes and cracked the window. She liked sleeping in a cool room. Only when everything was perfect did she climb into bed and pick up a hardback copy of Declan's first book, *Space Warrior*.

She didn't open it. She stroked the cover and smelled the pages. His bio was on the inside flap. She read it again, though she'd already committed it to memory.

Author DR Thomas lives in small-town Canada with his pet cat, Petunia. A mechanic by trade, he's given up working on cars to pursue his passion of crafting epic science fiction novels. He values his privacy and rarely makes public appearances.

"Rarely? How about never?" She snorted out a laugh. "Good thing his bio doesn't have his picture," she told the pretty space alien heroine on the book's cover. "He'd be swamped with overeager fans wanting to spend time with a silver-fox like him." He was so sexy; he ranked even above Sam Elliott or Mark Harmon as Gibbs.

She reread the book blurb and opened the cover once more. She stroked the cartoon avatar where Declan's face should be. Since she'd met him, she saw the resemblance between the little alien and the real man. She'd never look at his avatar without smiling now that she knew the truth.

He really was a mechanic. He'd been so startled by her appearance that he'd blushed a bit. He seemed…not shy exactly, more awkward, like herself. Of course, she had come on strong, and he wasn't used to being identified. She closed her eyes, picturing his long, lean thighs, and those gorgeous brown eyes. So alluring. She could have stared into them for hours.

OMG! She knew where her favorite author lived! A giggle escaped her. She walked past his house every day on her way to and from work. They were almost neighbors, there were only a dozen blocks between them. Another giggle.

She sipped her tea. She was so wound up; she would need a gallon of tea to get to sleep. Good thing it was still early. A warm, romantic feeling stole over her. Sweet heaven, she had a crush on a man she'd talked to for less than ten minutes. She was a total nut.

Chuckling to herself, she turned to chapter one and immediately became a flirty heroine aboard a generation ship, hurtling towards the stars, unaware of the violent species in hot pursuit and bent on destruction. When the book's secondary main character, a rough and tumble space cowboy, appeared, he looked exactly like Declan. Oh, for certain, the book's description was entirely different, but her overactive imagination turned herself into the main character and Declan into her cohort. Suddenly, she was extra eager to get deeper into the story.

She'd realized a couple years ago that as she aged, her favorite books brought different messages. The books changed with her perceptions of the world. This was entirely different because her favorite novel was morphing into something decidedly romantic and steamy. She wasn't going to get any sleep tonight. None!

She wondered when she'd see him again.

Chapter Six

Declan glared at his brothers. "This is ridiculous. You honestly expect me to wear a teddy bear costume? I'll sweat my butt off in this thing. It has to weight thirty pounds." Fluffy and purple, the plushie costume was an embarrassment. "What kind of crazy town throws a combination costume ball and Christmas Party? And why on December first? Can't I just go as a hobo, or maybe throw a sheet over my head and be a ghost?"

"Not this time," Ross, his oldest brother, said. "I flew in from Florida for this event. You'll wear a proper costume."

"Easy for the guy with the Zorro costume to say. How is it that you're Zorro, Tom's Iron Man, and I'm a damned stuffed animal? This is insane. Certifiable." He did not want to do this. He wanted to stay home. Alone. If he finished the books he'd checked out last month, he could go to see Cynthia. Maybe ask her on a date. He hadn't had much chance to get in since they'd talked a few weeks ago. He was itching to see her again.

"Your librarian might be there," Tom said.

"Drop it," Declan ordered. He didn't need this discussion. Not one bit.

"It seems, our little brother can't talk to the super-sexy, hot librarian. Complete with the dark and stereotypical glasses. You know, the ones she'll take off just before she takes you to bed—"

"Shut it!" Declan interrupted Tom. "I'll wear the damn costume if you'll just shut up."

"I knew I'd goad him into coming," Tom whispered loudly.

Brothers. Sometimes they were more trouble than they were worth. "Ross, when are you moving up here?" He posed the question to turn their attention from him.

"I don't know. I'm almost ready to retire. I've got the money, but I'm only fifty-four. It seems early. I'd need something to do since I won't be working. It's not like I have a family. The boys are busy with their careers. There's nothing here for me. You two turds aren't enough to bring me here for good. A visit I'll do, but not long-term."

"Are you happy at NASA?" Declan asked, struggling into the bottom half of his purple bear suit and wondering how he'd let them talk him into this.

"I'm not unhappy," Ross answered. "Are you happy? How's retirement for you? How's the secret writing gig working out?"

"You know what, aside from wanting a woman in my life, I am happy. I love tinkering on cars for friends and neighbors. It brings in a bit of extra money for me. I'm content." Never mind the royalties he received from the sale of five block-buster novels, most of which sat in the bank untouched.

He'd written the first story after watching a horrible sci-fi movie and figured he could do better. He devoured a few books on writing, and the story had practically flown out of him. He'd found an agent at the third agency he submitted to. She had gotten him a book deal within a month. It was the classic rags to riches story, and he knew he was damned lucky to get a contract for his first book.

Books one and two were easy. He'd argued with his editor about the plot of book three and had struggled to write it because he'd had to alter the plot. It turned out to be his most popular book. It seemed that, unlike his editor, people liked space dragons. Books four and five were okay. Not too hard to write. But book six? Book six was a total disaster. He was overdue to submit. He'd gotten two extensions from his publisher, and he had barely even started it yet. For the first time in his ten-year career, he was blocked. Totally and completely without an idea on how to wrap up the series. But he wasn't sharing all that with his brothers. He'd continue to sit at his desk and pretend he was working. Maybe if he sat there long enough, the story would come to him.

"Well, think about moving in. The house is more than big enough for the three of us. Plus, there's room for your boys when they come home to visit. It's a win-win all the way around. Seriously, consider the idea." He pulled on the top half of his costume and zipped it up. Thank heaven for front zippers. The costume was embarrassing enough that he didn't want to ask for help. Furry head under his arm, he headed for the door.

The Winterfest Bash was in full swing when they arrived. A twelve-foot tree lit with glittering ornaments and multi-colored lights dominated one corner. Snowflakes hung from fishing line off the ceiling. Snowmen, elves, and jolly Santas decorated the wall. The community center had been decorated for the children's party earlier in the day. It made sense to keep the whimsical décor up for the adult event. It was a Christmas lover's fantasy come to life.

Loud chatter filled the spaces between the songs blasted out by the deejay. Dancers swirled around the floor doing everything from a slow waltz to something which resembled a chicken having a seizure. He wasn't much of a dancer, but even he was better than that guy. He stifled a laugh.

He greeted the few people he was friends with and headed to the bar for a soda. He was sweating already. He nearly tripped over his furry feet when he noticed Cynthia at the makeshift bar. He paused to muster his courage.

"Can I buy you a drink?" he asked, stepping up beside her. She was glorious. She wore a circlet of leaves like a crown and a pale blue toga clung to her curves. Her normal updo was missing; her glorious auburn hair tumbled down her back, past her shoulders, in a sumptuous riot of curls he wanted to bury his hands in. He nearly swallowed his tongue when she smiled at him.

"Do I know you?" she asked, her eyes sparkled.

"We're acquaintances. You work at the library. I'm a patron." The words flew out; there was something freeing about being incognito.

"I see. And does that make it safe to have a drink with a stranger?" Her smile morphed from happy to flirtatious. Had she been drinking? She was never this outgoing with him. He liked the change.

"I will pay for your drink and never touch it." He turned toward the bartender. "Hi, Earl, can I have a ginger ale and whatever the lovely lady desires. Please and thank you."

Earl looked at Cynthia.

"Cola, please."

"Not drinking tonight?" he asked, wanting to continue their conversation.

"I'm not much of a drinker. The occasional wine. I'm more a tea granny, though I'm not actually a granny."

"And certainly not old enough to be a grandmother," he tried flattery.

Her laughter rippled down his body, ramping up the heat in his costume. He was going to combust if he wasn't careful. "Maybe I'll have a water too, Earl. With a straw. This suit is crazy hot. Just like this lovely lady." He winked and realized there was no way she'd see it. He tipped Earl and drank his water.

"Flattery? And a drink? Be still my beating heart." She rolled her eyes, making him laugh. "Who are you when you're not wearing that suit?"

"I'm hoping to be your cuddle bear." *Oh, God, the cornball lines. Where were they coming from?* He was making an ass of himself. For a man who made an extremely good living with his words, he sucked using them in person.

"And if I already have a cuddle bear?" she teased, sending his pulse skyrocketing.

"Do you?" he tried to keep his disappointment hidden.

"No. But I'm waiting for someone who I hope will fill the cuddle bear roll once I get to know him better." She turned and scanned the room.

Was it too much to hope she meant him? They'd talked a time or two, and she'd seemed shyly interested, especially after their last conversation on his driveway. What if the person she waited for wasn't him? Dammit. In that case, he'd stay with her until his rival showed up and find out what the competition was like.

"Well then, I shall keep you company until he arrives. Would you care to dance? Though I warn you, I'm not much of a dancer, and this suit is probably going to make it worse."

Laughing, she offered her hand. "Sure, why not? Lead me to the dance floor."

The deejay was playing a rowdy classic rock song. He led her to the center of the floor and tried his best not to look like an idiot while they danced. Her smile was infectious, and she moved beautifully. Not in any conventional dance step. More a gentle swaying and swiveling that led his mind and body straight to an erotic place.

The song morphed into Bryan Adams, *Everything I Do*. She gave him a questioning look.

"I'd love to," he answered the unspoken question and opened his arms. She stepped inside his embrace and he pulled her close, careful not to make it too close. He kept a respectful distance between them. One hand on her hip, the other holding her hand as he danced them slowly around the community center's dance floor.

"I love this song." She sighed. "So romantic."

"It is nice." Inching closer, he started to croon the lyrics along with the music surrounding them. It felt like he'd fallen through time and space, landing in heaven. They moved together around the floor; she anticipated his moves.

"I thought you couldn't dance?" Her voice was breathless, and she licked her lips, nearly bringing him to his overheated knees.

"Before tonight, without you, I couldn't. I swear. This is all you." Whew. That was a better line than saying she was hot, and he meant it too. She gave him grace, and in this stupid bear suit, he was suave and confident.

She laughed and stepped closer. "Thank you," she whispered.

His body went rock hard, and he barely kept from stumbling. They danced song after song, not once separating. They ignored the beat of the fast numbers and swayed together in a dark corner. The evening was perfect.

"This one's for the guy in the purple bear suit," the deejay announced.

Lonesome Loser began playing.

He made a sound of disgust. "Stupid brothers."

"Ignore them." She leaned her head on his shoulder, and the world faded away. There was nothing left but the two of them.

Chapter Seven

Cynthia couldn't believe how well her bear danced. They moved together perfectly. She should ask his name, but the thrill of dancing with a stranger was enticing. After a while, she forgot to watch for Declan and lost herself in the stranger's arms. His voice was vaguely familiar, but muffled by the suit. Buried beneath the myriad of scents in the room, she detected something that reminded her of Declan, something fresh and outdoorsy. She scanned the room but couldn't see him. Could the attentive man inside the bear suit be Declan?

After ten songs—yes, she was counting—his brothers played that song poking fun at him; it could have broken the mood, the sexual tension between them, but it didn't. They danced on and on. "You must be sweating in that costume."

"I am. I'm dying for a drink, but I don't want to let you out of my arms." Truth rang in his voice. It should be a total line, but her heart heard something more.

"Let's get some water," she stepped back, immediately missing the closeness they'd shared.

"What if I don't want to?" he asked, taking her hand and placing it in his elbow.

"Come on, bear, I need a drink and you do too. We can dance more later. After we hydrate. Dehydration can be dangerous."

"Dancing with you is dangerous," he countered.

Man, he was something with the bad lines. But it wasn't offensive, just a bit awkward. Like Declan always seemed awkward around her, like she felt around him. She froze in her tracks. Declan hadn't shown up yet; she scanned the room to make sure she hadn't missed his arrival. She was struck again by the idea that her cuddle bear could be Declan. She tugged him toward the bar. "Drink time."

She ordered them both sodas and water. She chugged down her water, and he sipped his through a straw. "Aren't you going to take off that head?" She really, really wanted him to show himself.

"And break the magical spell between us? That would be tragic."

She laughed; she couldn't help herself. "Those lines are tragic."

His laugh was deep and low. It sent shivers racing down her spine. Suddenly she was way overheated. She fanned herself. "You have a great laugh."

"Thank you." He finished his water and soda and offered his hand. "Shall we dance, beautiful lady?"

Dang, she wished she could be certain it was Declan inside the costume. There was just enough distortion through the suit that she had a sliver of doubt. No matter, she was going to pretend this was him and enjoy every second of dancing with the man of her dreams and fantasies.

She adored how he treated her carefully, but not like she was made of glass. He was polite and kind, despite his bad lines. She was enjoying herself more than she had in years.

♥♥♥

The dance had been on Saturday. Today was Monday. She was still caught up in a romantic haze thinking that her cuddle bear had been Declan. She felt ridiculously like a teenager again. She wandered around the library, humming classic rock love ballads under her breath. She found herself giggling more than once. She spent an hour tidying the library's largest section, romance. She read the back of every book, smiled at every cover, and searched for a story about love with a masked stranger. Really, all she was doing was waiting for Declan to arrive. He was in most Mondays and she wanted to find out if he was her bear.

By Wednesday, she was getting desperate.

Friday had her opening the library records and searching for his phone number. Realizing what she was doing, she clicked out of the program and went for lunch.

And what if they were both her cuddle bear?

She was being ridiculous. Pining away for someone she didn't know. Because, really, what were the chances of her purple bear being Declan? She was losing her mind. She was supposed to be an adult, not a lovestruck teenager.

Chapter Eight

Declan sat at his computer and started typing. For the first time in nearly two years, the words were coming. The day after the dance, he had a glimmer of an idea for a plot. Quickly, he jotted it down. As he typed, more and more details and plot items sprang to mind until his fingers couldn't keep up with his brain.

Six days later, he was still keyed up, invigorated. Passionate. All because he'd spend a couple hours dancing with Cynthia. He almost couldn't believe that he'd gotten so wrapped up that he'd forgotten they were in public. He was an idiot. But a productive one. His massive writer's block had exploded under the tender weight of Cynthia's embrace.

It was likely that his editor wasn't going to like him bringing book three's dragons back into the story, nor was he going to like the heavy romantic undertones that were developing for his heroine. Tough cookies. This was how the story wanted to be told, and he was writing it that way.

He'd worry about his agent's opinion later. Much later, after the book was written and submitted, because he was inspired and had learned that his muse was fickle. Very very fickle.

He barely slept; he only ate when Tom shoved food under his nose and complained that Declan needed to quit fiddling on the computer and get a life. It had been six days since he'd showered. He was exhausted and energized. Finally, he fell asleep at his desk. He didn't know how long he slept, but his back ached and he had the worst kink in his neck. After a soak in the tub, he felt refreshed and ready to go again.

He hopped into his desk chair with a grin. Time to get back to his novel. He'd already had two extensions on his submission date. If he missed this one, which was due in three weeks, he'd lose the contract and have to pay back the advance. Since the dance, he'd managed to write fifteen chapters, about forty thousand words. Since every other book in the series was one hundred and ten thousand words, he was a bit short. He wasn't a fast writer, he agonized over every word, but since the dance, his mind had stories demanding to get out.

The trouble was, he was tired of the world he had created and wanted to move on to a new series. He pushed aside the reality that his agent nixed more dragons telling him that he was no Anne McCaffrey. Plus, his rebellious female lead wanted those dragons. His subconscious had been shoving them at him since book two. He finally incorporated them in a limited capacity into book three. Then, at his editor's request, he'd kept their role small, but now that the ship had docked at the character's future home, he felt the dragons were integral in the finale.

"What the hell do I do now?" he mumbled.

"Bro, you taking to yourself?" Ross poked his head in through the open office door.

"Yes." He sighed. "I should be writing, instead I'm wool gathering." He pushed his rolling chair away from the desk and leaned back.

"I can't believe you are DR Thomas. I've read all your books and every short story you published in magazines. Why didn't you tell us? We're your brothers." He slouched in the chair opposite Declan's oak desk. "Seriously, why didn't you tell us?"

"Look at you," he waved vaguely, "You're a mathematician for NASA. Tom's a carpenter with specialty items in high-end shops the world round. I'm just a grunt mechanic. Don't misunderstand. I love my work. Both the tinkering with cars and writing books. I just felt that…"

"Oh man, you're not hearing Uncle Ralph's words in your head, are you? Just because his dick-headed son is literally a brain surgeon, it doesn't mean there's anything shameful about less glamorous jobs like being a mechanic or writing books. The world needs more stories and more readers to devour them. I've managed to get at least a dozen of my coworkers hooked on your books. One dude calls them brain-crack because they're so addicting. Three guys have started writing fan fiction using your world. And I didn't even know you wrote them." The last words were said with good-natured ribbing.

"Nerds." Declan laughed.

"They are total nerds. But if you can impress guys with brains that big, you're doing okay. Besides, don't you have four best-seller titles?"

"Eight if you count national and international differently." He couldn't help but grin. Book one had been a hit, but it wasn't until book two that he'd hit the bestseller lists.

"Lay it out straight for me. I know math, not words, but I am a problem solver. What issue are you dealing with?" He shifted in his chair and rested his feet on Declan's desk.

Declan lifted his own feet and leaned further back. "Dragons."

"I loved those dragons. Honestly, you don't use them enough. I'd like to see more. One of those fan fictions, and I read them no matter how poorly they're done, one of them focuses almost entirely on the dragons."

"My editor hates them."

"Screw you editor. Please your fans. What happens if your editor hates it?"

"I could lose my next contract. But I think I'm going to risk it. This deadline is screaming up way too fast. I'll be lucky to be done by January. What brings you by my office this late at night anyway?" It was pushing midnight, and he'd thought both brothers had gone to bed hours ago.

"I can't sleep. Listen, Tom and I are taking your librarian's friends out for drinks again tomorrow night. You should come along. We'll get them to invite her to join us. Maybe you can grow a pair and actually talk to her."

"Funny. Not."

"You danced the entire night with her. You like her, right?"

Tough question. Should he admit he was crazy attracted to Cynthia or keep his mouth shut? Either way, he was in for a world of teasing. "She seems nice." He chose a safe middle path.

"Nice? She's as hot as heck," Ross declared. "She's a librarian and with those sexy glasses." He licked his fingertip, touched his arm, and made a sizzling sound. "Hotness."

"I thought you liked the other one, the blonde? Remember her?" He should remember, he'd babbled all through dinner about how perfect she was. He couldn't even admit that Cynthia was, by far, the best looking of the trio.

"She's hot. I'll grant you that," Ross said. "All of them are. They could be centerfolds." He winced at the words, as if he knew they were inappropriate. "Seriously, they're beautiful, friendly. Did you know that Nora's a painter? A seriously good painter. So good I can barely even afford to consider buying them and I've got more than my share of money." In an abrupt turn of subject, he said, "You should come out with us. Even if you don't hit it off with what's her name, you can have a couple brewskis with us and chill. Relax that bookish brain and pretend you're human."

"I'll think about it."

"About what?" Tom strolled through the doorway and leaned against the wall.

"Coming for drinks with us tomorrow. But he's too big a wimp. He's too shy." His voice dripped mockery.

"You should totally come. She was all over you, caressing you with her eyes. She thinks you're some kind of superstar just because you write books. Seriously, what's with women?" Tom's ex had burned him badly. She'd dumped him. Not for a younger man, but for a younger couple. She was now living in a group marriage in San Francisco. A group marriage with seventeen children and ten adults, all living together. He didn't understand the lifestyle, but she seemed happy. Tom claimed she'd left him just because they couldn't conceive. But Declan suspected there was more to the failed marriage than his brother let on.

"Women are beautiful, intelligent creatures," Declan said. "Beautiful and terrifying."

"You need to get over being dumped at prom. Francine Boatman was nothing but a loser and slut. Plus, a total bitch for taking a dare and inviting you in the first place. She's not worth your time." Tom moved to sit on the other guest chair. "She never was."

"Honestly, I haven't thought of her for years. I'm just not good with single attractive women. If they're drop dead gorgeous and married, I can talk all day. But until I know they're married, not a peep passes these lips. I'm messed up. There's no getting around it. Going on a triple date with you guys would suck. I'd sit there, staring at Cynthia, my mouth full of wool, looking like a damned fool. No thanks."

"You've already had a full conversation with her. You are probably the most pathetic man on the planet," Tom threw down the challenge.

"Yup."

"Little baby Decky. Can't talk to girls," Ross teased. "Won't go on a date because someone might hurt his pretty little feelings. Boo hoo hoo."

"Can it." He knew what they were doing. Going back to their childhood. They'd been taken in as foster kids, one after the other, barely out of diapers. Declan was first. Then came Thomas, and finally Ross. When Declan was ten, their foster parents had adopted them, making them true brothers.

In all those years, and the years that followed, they had perfected teasing and goading each other. Eventually, it led to good-natured wrestling and often to caving in and doing what the others wanted. Since he wasn't up to a physical match this late at night, he caved.

"Fine. I'll go on your stupid date, and I'll look like an idiot. Get them to bring Cynthia. Now go to bed and let me write this book."

"Good night." In unison, they strode from the room.

"Told you we could talk him into it," Tom said.

Declan heard their high five.

Goofballs. His brothers were pests, but they meant well. He smiled and straightened in his chair. He had a date with Cynthia, and he hadn't even had to ask.

Grinning like a fool, he opened the document and began typing. If the heroine in his book happened to change from a flirty brunette to a sexy redhead, she could be fixed in edits, because all of a sudden, his muse flooded him with fresh inspiration. He was still typing when the morning sun brightened his office and his brothers began to stir upstairs.

Chapter Nine

Cynthia paced the library. It was quiet today. She was working alone because Friday was always dead. In the city, Fridays and weekends had always been busy. Here in Valley Springs, she could be closed on Friday and barely anyone would notice, except Maxine. She had every Friday off. Right now, she was holed up in the science section reading up on renewable resources. For someone who should have retired fifteen years ago, the septuagenarian was a force to be reckoned with.

The front bell chimed, and Cynthia whirled to face it. Her heart soared and then plummeted to her toes. "Hi, Greg." Greg was a regular; a year or two younger than Maxine, he came in every day for something new to read.

"She's in reference," Cynthia whispered when he drew close.

Greg blushed. It was adorable on a man his age. "I don't know what you're talking about," he blustered.

"Maxine. She's reading up on solar panels, or metal recycling, or something. She asks about you…" She left the words hanging. The pair would make an adorable couple. They both had dreams of living in an RV and travelling all through Canada and the United States. They were both attracted to the other and too shy to start anything. Somebody needed to give them a push.

Since she didn't have a man in her life, and was too shy to approach Declan, she might as well help them hook up. They were perfect for each other. Unlike her and Declan. The only thing they had in common was books. His books.

Her stomach rolled. She had a date tonight. Well, not a date exactly. She'd agreed to go to the pub with her friends and their dates. Declan would be there too. End of story.

So why was she so excited?

Abruptly, she realized Greg was saying something. "I'm sorry, Greg. I zoned out there."

"Do you think I should talk to her?" He jingled his keys in his pocket, the sound loud in the silence of the library.

"Didn't you used to work in green tech before you retired?" After he nodded agreement, she went on. "She's researching that type of stuff. Just walk in and notice what she's reading and make a comment. Strike up a conversation."

"I don't know. It's been twenty years since my wife passed, and longer since I asked anyone on a date."

"Just do it, Greg. Be brave. Chase your dream." If only it were that easy, she'd be sitting in Declan's living room having coffee and listening to him read his books.

Greg pushed out three staccato breaths. "I'm going in. Wish me luck."

She leaned over and kissed his cheek. "Go get her, tiger."

Greg strode toward Maxine, muttering under his breath. Cynthia laughed.

"What did he say that was so funny?"

She whirled around to face Declan. "Declan, hi. I didn't hear you come in. I was giving Greg a pep talk."

"Is he finally going to do it?" He seemed awed.

"I think so. He likes her so much, but he's afraid."

"Fear sucks." There was a wealth of feeling in Declan's voice. Far more than the simple statement should need.

"It sure does." How could she do anything but agree? She was fifty-three and scared to put herself out there, but also terrified she'd die a spinster. It would be okay if she could count on her roommates being there until the end, but both were actively seeking partners. Eve was even trying online dating. She shuddered just thinking about meeting up with a stranger for dinner.

They stood staring at each for a few minutes. Time ticked by until Cynthia's feet started to ache. If he wasn't going to speak, she had to. "Is there something I can help you with?"

"Did you want me to sign those books? Man, it feels crazy to ask that, like I'm a star or something, which I am not."

"Would you really? It's not weird at all. I love your books. I've gone to a ton of book fairs to get author autographs. I once stood in line for four hours to get a Nora Roberts autograph. I actually flew to Vegas to a writer's conference to get an autograph. You should see my collection. It's amazing!"

He backed up a step and put his hands up. "This isn't going to go all *Silence of the Lambs,* is it?" He winked.

She buried her face in her hands. "No." She looked up at him, hoping he didn't notice the heat in her face. "I'm sorry, I'm just, well, I do work here for a reason. I'm kind of a book nerd. Nothing excites me more than books."

"I'll remember that."

"Oh gosh." Would the world just open up and swallow her already, before she put another foot in her mouth. "Any-way," she dragged the word out. "My books are behind the checkout desk."

He followed her over, waiting patiently until she was behind the desk.

"Don't freak out. You know I'm a fan." She set her backpack on the desk and started unloading it. Hardcover and paperback copies of all his books and an eight-inch stack of magazines he had stories in. There were even CDs of his audiobooks.

"Wow."

She shrugged, trying not to be embarrassed. "I told you, I'm a fan. You're my favorite author." Okay, maybe it was weird that she had three copies of all the books. Four if you counted her e-reader, but he couldn't sign that. "Are you totally weirded out?"

His smile stole her breath. "Maybe a little bit. The only books I've ever autographed were for my agent and editor; and I did a few for a publisher's giveaway." He pulled a fancy gold pen from his pocket and flipped open the first paperback. "How do you spell your name?"

"You don't know how to spell Cynthia?" She blinked in surprise.

"I do, but I want to make sure it's spelled properly for you. My friend's wife spells Lori Lynn as Laurie Linne." He spelled each word. "To each his own, right? And I don't want to disappoint you."

She dictated her name for him as he wrote.

"There you go." He passed her the first book and picked up the second.

She read the inscription. *"Thanks to a chance meeting on the street, I met my number one and my favorite fan. All the best, DR Thomas."*

"Your number one fan?" she chuckled.

"You're the first fan I've ever met, that makes you officially number one." He handed over the book he'd just signed. "I never really thought about fans. I've done a lot of audio podcasts, and a number of radio interviews, but somehow, I've never connected that to reader fans. Don't get me wrong, I know readers who like my books are why I'm successful, I just never really put it all together." His brows pinched together. "I'm very grateful that people like my work. Thank you."

She hugged the book he'd signed to her chest. "No, thank you for signing, and for writing such fabulous books."

They stared at each other awkwardly.

"Is this going to be a thing?" he asked. "This staring without speaking because really, it weirds me out a bit."

"Me too." She swallowed down an awkward feeling that made her stomach churn. "I'm sorry. I'll try not to fangirl too much, if you'll tell me what book six is about."

He leaned in close like he was going to share a secret. She leaned in too. He smelled like mint and freshly showered man. Delicious. She sniffed discretely, memorizing the scent in case she never saw him again. He looked left and right, then left again. "My book is about…"

"Yes?" she asked breathlessly.

"I can't tell you."

She reared back. "What?" She slapped his arm playfully. "You jerk."

"All I can tell you is that it's going well. I was stuck before the Winterfest dance; then I had a flash of inspiration. I wrote nonstop for days. I barely got out of my chair. Last night, I wrote for ten hours straight. That's a long time for me. My legs totally cramped when I stood up."

"Is that how it works for you? Write the whole book in a rush?"

"No. I usually write a couple hours a day and then move to other stuff. Gardening, shoveling, fixing cars."

"Nice." She loved the insight into his process.

"How about you? Do you read a lot?"

"Hmm. Does a librarian read a lot?" She tapped her finger on her chin. "Let's see, last night I read *Space Warrior* from cover to cover." She yawned. "I might be a bit overtired this morning." *Space Warrior* was his first novel.

"You actually reread it?" He seemed astounded, and maybe flattered.

She hid a blush. "Okay, maybe that's the tenth or fifteenth time I've read it. So, sue me. I reread the entire series every year, and every time a new book in the series is released, I read the series from the start. I love your characters, and the stories draw me in like I'm living them." Why was she telling him this? She should be embarrassed, but she wasn't; because now that they'd met, he was surprisingly easy to talk to.

"That is so weird. I haven't read them cover to cover that many times and I wrote them. Your interest flatters me. Thank you."

"You're welcome. Now, go write that next book. I can't wait. Can I read it as you write it?" She couldn't stop the request.

"Nobody reads until it's done and edited."

"How soon is that? I'm not sure I can wait." She couldn't seem to shut up about how great he was. She was going to scare him off and then she'd be sitting in the pub alone tonight.

"Depends on the book. Book three came really fast. About half the time of book one, and a hundredth the time of this one. This one was killing me."

"Want to talk about it?" Motion to her left caught her eye. Maxine and Greg were headed their way, walking side by side. "Don't look now," she whispered. "Here they come."

Declan stepped aside so she could check out Maxine's books. "What are you to up to tonight?" she asked them.

Maxine blushed. "Greg is taking me to dinner in Whitefalls." Her smile was amazing.

"I finally got up the courage to ask her out," Greg said.

"I've been waiting for five years." Her tone was gently chiding. "I had about given up hope. I decided this morning that I was going to ask him." She sounded slightly scandalized at the idea of asking a man out, but she smiled at Cynthia. "Don't wait forever. If you see a man you like, ask him out. Life's too short." She picked up her books walked out hand in hand with Greg.

They watched them go.

"Well, that was interesting," she said when she finally got over her shock.

"They're quite the pair. I've talked to both of them a lot. But she's right. Life is short." His Adam's apple bobbed. "Will you go to the pub with me tonight?"

"Aren't we doing that already?" She wasn't sure what he meant.

"I mean officially. I can pick you up at home, or meet you there. I'm asking you on a date, not just a tag along." He swallowed again. "I've wanted to ask you for a while."

Holy crap! She hadn't realized he'd even known she was alive before she'd accosted him on his driveway, and he wanted to ask her out.

OMG! Her favorite author asked her on a date. The hottest guy in town to boot.

She felt like a teenager, not someone old enough to be a grandmother. Her stomach jumped and her pulse skyrocketed. Her palms got sweaty and her knees threatened to buckle.

Breathe, Cyn, breathe.

"I'd like that very much, thank you."

"Shall I pick you up?"

She thought about the question. It was a weird and sometimes dangerous world, but she felt safe with him. Her friends would be there, as would his brothers. "Sure." She gave him her address and phone number. "I'll be ready for seven."

"I'll be there." He signed the rest of her books and said goodbye. As she returned the books to her backpack, she heard him whistling. The cheery tune stuck in her head for hours.

Chapter Ten

Still wet from his shower, Declan heard Tom calling him. "What do you want? I'm shaving." The door between his bedroom and bathroom opened, and Tom rushed in. "Aren't you ready to go? We want to be there before the ladies. Hurry up."

"I'll meet you there. Go on without me." He hadn't told his brothers about his date with Cynthia. He kept running his razor over his face. He wanted to be perfectly smooth in case he managed to steal a kiss.

"You're not bailing, are you? I swear…"

"Give me some privacy, man. I'll be there. I'm picking up Cynthia at home and if you don't leave so I can get dressed, I'll be late." He finished shaving, removed the towel from around his waist, and hung it neatly on the bar. He strode past his brother to his dresser, not caring that he was naked.

"I'm leaving. You better show up…" His voice was heavy with warning.

"I'll be there. Go. Away." Nothing like sharing your house with two brothers. He'd been living with Tom since Tom retired from his career as a teacher. Now they were trying to get Ross to retire. Family belonged together, or at least close to each other.

Their adoptive parents had passed several years ago. Aside from Ross's two adult sons, the three of them were all the family that was left. Both sons were serving in the military and were barely ever home. There was no reason for Ross not to move into Declan's place which was now the family home. The house was massive. Five bedrooms, a three-car garage, and an enormous workshop out back where Tom did his woodworking and carpentry. Tom lived in the walkout basement suite. There was plenty of room for another person.

Ten years ago, after his first big book deal, Declan had moved to Valley Springs on a whim. At the time, there were precious few houses for sale. When he couldn't find what suited him, he'd purchased three small, dilapidated homes side by side, all owned by the same slum-lord. After helping the current tenants find new places to live, he'd had them torn down and used any material that was recyclable to build his new home. Tom had been his primary contractor and had fallen in love with Valley Springs and moved in before the house was finished.

He stood staring into his closet. There wasn't much to choose from. Two suits that he used for weddings and funerals, more well-worn jeans than one man needed, and a couple of button-down shirts. He'd been to the library hundreds of times, maybe only ninety since he'd noticed Cynthia two years ago; she'd be used to seeing him in jeans and a Henley. He wanted to do better. This was a date after all, and he intended to impress her with something besides his writing prowess.

He put on his newest jeans, a plaid dress shirt, and his best casual shoes. Comfortable ones; not the monsters he wore with his suits. He combed his hair, slapped on some aftershave, and looked at himself in the mirror. Not bad for someone his age. He could pass for forty-five rather than his actual fifty-two. He looked good. Handsome, if he said so himself. Far better looking than his adopted brothers. He laughed at his himself. They were all handsome men, and he wasn't ashamed to admit it.

He stood for a moment, debating between his pickup truck and his car. He'd rather drive the truck, it was his favorite, but it was a four by four and quite high. If Cynthia wore a skirt, *please let her wear a skirt,* she might have trouble climbing into the truck. Besides that, he hadn't taken it for a test drive since he'd repaired the rad.

Car it was. He snatched the keys off the hook by the garage door and headed out. The Dodge Charger was several years old—okay, over a decade—but it ran like a dream, and he kept it body and engine in top condition. Working on cars had been his dream; now it was his hobby and a great break from writing.

Less than five minutes later, he strode up to Cynthia's door. She opened it before he could knock.

"Oh, hi," he blurted. *Suave.* She was glorious. Her hair shone under the porch light. She was backlit by the entry light; her hair shone like a halo of rose gold. Somewhere between strawberry blonde and light mahogany, it curled softly past her shoulders, begging him to touch it. She wore a short, mid-thigh, black dress that hid more than it revealed, but it made him want to uncover all the secrets it shielded. Her lips were enticingly red, her high-heeled boots made her legs seem longer and sexy. He damn near had to clutch his chest, she was giving him a heart attack. So much for the story that you lost interest in women and sex as you aged. He felt like a randy teenager. Horny, stunned, and speechless. *Say something. Channel your inner cuddle bear.*

"You look incredible. That dress is amazing. I mean, you always look nice, but that dress is…wow!" She was going to think he was a total idiot. "Let me help you with your jacket, if you're ready." Her blush was sweet and becoming.

"I'm ready to go. Thanks for coming to pick me up, and you look quite dapper yourself. That blue plaid suits you." She handed him her coat and turned around so he could help her slide her arms in.

He wondered if the gesture was too old fashioned and decided he didn't care. Cynthia accepted it and that's all that mattered. He held the outer door while she stepped outside and locked up. "It's a bit slippery with the snow, can I help you to the car?" He offered his elbow.

She looked at him and wrinkled her nose. Just when he was certain he'd overdone the chivalry, she smiled. "Sure, why not? I'd like that."

He led her down the walk and held open the car door for her. He closed it firmly once she was settled.

"Oh, it's nice and warm in here," she commented as they buckled up.

"I keep her in the garage. I left her running while I went to the door; I didn't want you to catch a chill." *Would his mouth never shut up?*

"I appreciate it. The temperature really dropped since I walked home. You weren't outside today."

Had she noticed that he was often outside when she walked past? *Not good.* "I was in the office, writing. I lost track of time." He wanted to bang his forehead on the steering wheel. "Well, I guess I just admitted to watching you. I hope that's not too creepy."

Her laugh rang out, light and sunshiny. "Well, maybe just a little. I thought it was weird at first, but you never spoke to me, so I decided it must be a coincidence. I guess not." She shrugged eloquently, and he pulled away from the curb.

"Whew. It wasn't my intention to be weird."

"Why were you out front so often?"

"Honestly, I was trying to work up the balls, er courage, to talk to you. I'm not good with women." *And there went his errant mouth. Again.*

"Really? You talk to Maxine all the time. I've seen you chatting with a lot of women at the library."

"Were *you* watching *me*?" he teased.

"Maybe a little." Her pink cheeks were adorable and made him want to put her at ease. He didn't want her to feel uncomfortable around him.

"Let's make a deal. No more covert ops. Let's just talk to each other, and maybe call or text sometime. We can be upfront about our interest." He stopped at a stop sign and waggled his eyebrows at her. "And I'll be less creepy." He was actually flirting with her, awkwardly, but flirting.

"I can't call or text, I don't have your number. Apparently, it's a national secret or some kind of elite artist thing."

He drove through the intersection and stopped at the side of the road to pull out his phone and shoot her a text.

Her face lit with surprise when her phone chimed. "Now, you have my number. Use it anytime. Day or night."

"Can I ask you author secrets?"

"Nope. The plot is secret, even from me at this point. I'm making it up as I go along." They laughed together as he pulled back onto the street.

He opened the pub door to a cacophony of noise. Clinking glasses, laughter, instrumental Christmas carols. Everyone was in a jovial mood. People greeted Cynthia as they walked through the busy pub to the table with their friends. She was very popular in town. Very few people acknowledged him. His fault, he was too much an introvert and liked being at home. Cynthia wasn't shy, but she did seem politely reserved, as she did in the library.

He almost laughed at the irony of two introverts coming together over the unspoken word. He was going to mention it to her, but they had arrived at their table.

"Yay, they finally made it," Eve teased. "Pull up a chair."

Two chairs remained, side by side at the crowded round table. Eve sat between his brothers, but a bit closer to Tom. Nora sat close to Ross. Since they were alternating boy-girl, he pulled out the chair next to Ross and held it while Cynthia removed her jacket and sat. He took the seat next to her. She smelled glorious, like sunshine and flowers.

The Ram's Head Pub was hopping. Every table was full. It was a good thing the others had arrived early or they'd have been out in the cold. He looked around the pub. He'd been here a few times and was always impressed by its light, clean looks. Solid tables, cartoony art prints on the bright walls. It was decorated to the nines for Christmas. A sparkling tree in the corner by the door and colored lights strung up everywhere. He loved the transition from watering hole to Christmas wonderland. Garland and glass balls hung from the ceiling.

He knew the drinks were always good, and there was a large variety of beer on tap. The food was fresh and tasty. And tonight, tonight the company was exquisite.

A jazz trio was playing Christmas tunes in the corner and somehow managing to keep the music low enough for conversation. A few dancers whirled around the small dance floor next to the bandstand. Interwoven with the holiday atmosphere were the smells of good whiskey and delicious food. Sitting beside Cynthia, the pub was pure heaven.

"Hey, everyone," Cynthia said. She got a chorus of responses.

"What took you so long?" Eve asked. "We've been here for twenty minutes." She winked like she was in on some big secret.

"No reason. I waited for Declan, and we came right over. Just because you were super eager to get here and left early, it doesn't mean we were late." She stuck her tongue out at her friends.

"We're late because I was late. I let the car warm up so Cynthia could ride in comfort." Not true, but Cynthia's red cheeks told him that she didn't like her friend's teasing, and he had to defend her.

Her friends both sighed, and his brothers rolled their eyes. "Dec, you're making us look bad."

Time to rub it in. "I can't help it if you didn't consider the weather and ask to pick up your dates." His statement caused a round of good-natured bickering.

Cynthia leaned in and nudged him with her shoulder. "I love the way you guys banter. It's kind of like what these two and I do." She gestured at Eve and Nora with her thumb. "Only you guys are way meaner."

"It's all in good fun. I figure if you can't laugh at yourself, you don't have a sense of humor."

"I like that. I do try not to take myself too seriously. Though sometimes it is difficult."

"Everyone seems to know you." He switched topics.

She laughed. "You'd be surprised how many people in this town rely on the library. I'm actually quite shocked. Patron numbers in the city were declining; here I think we're actually gaining strength. I see a lot of people every week. We've got four book clubs."

"They treat you like a friend." The dynamics fascinated him as a person and as a writer. "But you seem, I don't know, reserved with them."

"I'm not that outgoing. The library is my domain. Books are my passion. I adore helping people. At the library, I can talk with them, without putting myself on the line. Does that make sense? Otherwise, I keep to myself."

"I get it. I have a few good friends but not many." Time to change the subject from his awkward personality. "I saw you at the Winterfest dance."

Chapter Eleven

Cynthia paused at his comment. "You were at the Winterfest dance? I didn't see you. What were you wearing?" Time for him to confess to being a bear…if it had been him.

"Ah, it's a secret. I was incognito. Can't have fans accosting me in public."

"Low blow." She laughed. "That was…it was an unusual circumstance. I'd only figured it out hours before and then you didn't come into the library. Where had you been; you didn't come in for two weeks." *Way to reveal the depths of your stalking desperation.*

"Writing. Sometimes it pulls me in and everything else disappears. After the dance, I was…I don't know, inspired, I guess. I started writing, and it just kept coming. I expect my ability to get caught up in fiction makes me a terrible roommate."

"Never apologize for creative genius. I've got two artist roommates. I've lost track of the number of times

I've been abandoned mid-conversation when their muse appeared. I think if you're in a relationship with an artist, you have to be prepared to sit alone sometimes."

"And are you in a *relationship*?" he asked.

"I'm not dating anyone. Though I thought I connected with a gentleman at the dance the other night. Except he didn't reveal his identity, or ask for my number. I should have gotten his, I guess."

"Unless he's an idiot, you'll be hearing from him. And if you don't, he doesn't deserve you anyway."

Cyn considered his words. He was probably right. "And is there a Mrs. Famous Author, or perhaps a future Mrs.?" She suspected not, since he lived with his brothers, but before they took this thing any further, she wanted to be one hundred percent certain.

"No! Of course not. I wouldn't have asked you out if there had been. Has that happened to you?" He sounded appalled.

"My ex-husband dumped me for his secretary. His much younger secretary."

"Holy shoot. Who does that? The man was an idiot. Who could dump a woman like you? Smart, pretty, a good dancer, kind." He shook his head. "He was an idiot, and a jerk."

"You've got that right." He thought she was a good dancer. Sweet.

Wait! They had never danced together. Unless of course he was the bear.

"How do you know I'm a good dancer? I've never danced with you." She had him now. "Dec, were you being a stalker creep at the dance and watching me?"

"Yeah, Dec, were you being a creep at the dance?" Ross asked.

"Dude!" Declan reached across and punched his brother in the shoulder.

"Were you creeping on our friend?" Nora asked, sounding angry. "I didn't see you there. Were you hiding?"

"No, I was not watching Cynthia dancing with the bear at the dance. I was the damn bear." He turned to her. "Sorry, I was going to tell you."

She started to giggle and clamped a hand over her mouth. She'd suspected it was him, and she knew he hadn't meant to give himself away. Her giggle turned to chuckles then to outright laughter. The more she laughed, the darker his expression grew. That made her laugh harder.

"That's it, I'm done here. Someone please give Cynthia a ride home." He grabbed his coat and strode from the bar.

Abruptly, her mood sobered. She hadn't meant to offend him. "Declan, wait!" She rushed after him. Outside, she turned left and right, shivering in the frigid north wind. An engine roared and his car raced past her, fishtailing down the street. Behind the wheel, his face looked like thunder.

"That went well." She turned to go inside. "You have to fix this. Now." She returned to the table. Her companions looked solemn.

"Sorry about that," Ross said.

"Yeah. I am so sorry," Nora added. "I didn't mean to create an issue."

"Do you want to know what the stupid thing is? I knew he was the bear all along. Do you have any idea how hard it is for me to open up and befriend a man? Do you?" She glared at her friends.

"If it's any consolation, Dec's got the same problem. He's been in the best mood ever since the dance. He's wanted to talk to you for ages," Tom said.

Ross apologized again, promising to keep his mouth shut in the future. "Do you want me to take you home?"

"Hell no. I'm going to his place to apologize for our idiot friends and for laughing. I may never forgive any of you." She gave them another round of glares as she picked up her jacket. "Call me a taxi." Valley Springs had no Uber or Lyft drivers.

Any other day, her friends would have replied by saying, "You're a taxi." It was a tribute to her friends' apology that they said nothing. Eve pulled out her phone and punched in numbers as Cynthia walked away.

Luck was with her, a taxi pulled up just as she stepped outside. Maybe it wasn't the one Eve called, she had no idea, but she took it anyway. She didn't have Declan's address, so she directed the cab which turns to take.

"You didn't know the address, so this isn't your place. Do you want me to wait here?" the thirtyish male driver asked.

She debated the question. "You know what? I'd appreciate that. If I get in the house, you can leave." She paid him and tipped him well before climbing out of the cab.

She stared up at the house. There were no lights on, but there were fresh vehicle tracks leading into the garage, and no footprints on the sidewalk. He was here, and they were going to talk.

She wasn't some shrinking flower or nervous virgin. She was a competent woman with a lifetime of experience to fall back on. She'd dealt with all kinds of people in the library, though there weren't usually any confrontations. She could do this. "Put on your big girl panties, Cynthia. You've got this."

Careful not to slip in the snow, she hurried up the walk and pounded on the door. She waited thirty seconds and pounded again. After the fourth round of knocks, the door flew open.

"Haven't you guys done enough damage?" Declan demanded before the door was fully open. "Oh. Cynthia."

"Can I come in?"

He stood there, one hand on the doorknob, the other on the wall beside the doorframe. He didn't say anything. He just looked furious. Brows scrunched up; mouth turned down. Arms stiff enough his muscles bulged.

Nothing ventured, nothing gained. She pushed past him into the house. "We need to talk."

He shut the door and stood facing her, arms crossed over his chest, his face pinched into a frown. "Go ahead. Talk."

Rather than speak, she slipped out of her boots and hung her jacket in the hall closet, reaching around him to do so. She dropped her purse in the corner and padded, in her stocking feet, down the short hallway to the living room.

One end was dominated by a fireplace and bookcases, the other opened into an empty room, presumably the dining area. The empty room would be the perfect place for an oversized tree, preferably live. Two enormous leather couches lay along the side walls. The couches were dark brown, the carpet a soft beige. The walls were bare of everything except one Picasso reproduction; *The Scream*. Fitting for this moment.

"By all means, come in."

Oh, he was pouting. "Look, Declan. I'm not getting any younger, and neither are you." She swallowed the lump forming in her throat. It hit her stomach with a thump that sent enormous butterflies dancing in a hurricane. She hadn't been in a personal confrontation since her last fight with her ex. This was hard.

She closed her eyes and took a deep breath. "I apologize for laughing. I wasn't laughing at you. Well, I was, sort of. I was laughing at the look on your brothers' faces when you confessed to being the bear. I think they were shocked you admitted it. I suspected it was you. I *wanted* him to be you."

Declan's shoulders relaxed slightly. Good, she was getting through to him.

"Rabid fangirl aside, I like you. I've been attracted to you since I saw you in the library two years ago. Finding out you are my favorite author was a bonus, but it isn't important. You could be nothing more than a backyard mechanic and you'd still be a nice guy. The guy I can barely talk to. The guy I've been mustering up the courage to ask out. The man I want to get to know better."

She paced a circle around the coffee table and stopped to jab him in the chest with her finger. "It's like this. I'm a bit old school. In my day, women weren't the aggressors in a courtship. We waited to be asked out. Ugh. I sound like I'm ninety, not barely past fifty." She shook her head. "Anyway. This is me apologizing to you, asking you out on a date."

He was silent so long she was sure he'd reject her. Finally, he spoke. "You knew it was me in the suit?"

"Seriously? I make a speech about my feelings, and you're stuck on me knowing you were in the bear suit? You infuriate me, Declan Foxx." She forced herself to breathe slowly and not get angry. "Okay, maybe I didn't know it was you. I suspected it was you. I wanted it to be you." She resumed pacing. "That night was one of the most magical nights of my life. I spent it wrapped up in the arms of a kind and gentle man who tried his best to make me happy. Something about that bear reminded me of you. So yes, in my head you were the purple cuddle bear. Even if that bear had turned out to be another man, in my mind, in my heart, I was dancing with you. Deal with it."

"Cynthia."

"What?" she snapped.

He took a fast step toward her. They were almost nose to nose. "Shut up so I can kiss you." He swooped in and pressed his lips to hers, stealing her breath. She wrapped her arms around his neck, drawing him closer. Her hips thrust forward against him and came smack dab against the evidence of his desire.

She giggled. God help her, she couldn't stop herself. This wonderful man was aroused by her. It was beyond comprehension.

Declan leaned back. "Cyn, this is not the time for laughter. I'm not the most experienced man on the planet, so give me a break."

"Dec, I don't give a crap about your previous conquests. I'm just thrilled that you react to me like this." She squeezed his erection. "I've waited two years for a conversation with you. I'm done waiting." She backed up and grabbed his hands in hers. "Which way to the bedroom?"

Laughing, he scooped her in his arms and carried her up the stairs, like a young stud. He barely lost his breath at all. "Holy crap. I wasn't expecting that," she whispered when he stood her beside his bed and kicked the door shut.

"Before tonight, you never said a dozen words to me, and now you can't stop talking. Are you going to talk all the way through this?" he teased.

Laughter bubbled out of her. "Honestly? Probably. I'm done being nervous around you."

"What changed that?" he asked, skimming his fingers up and down her arms, bringing her entire body alive with need.

She fumbled with his belt buckle. "I don't know, lust? Something deeper? Knowing you're a good man? There's a lot going on in my head and heart right now."

"Fangirl moment?" he teased, placing small kisses along the neckline of her dress, moving toward the back zipper. "God, did I tell you how hot this dress makes me?"

"Declan?"

"Yeah?" He pulled the zipper down with his teeth.

"Shut up and kiss me." She whirled in a circle, taking him with her, and pushed him onto his back on the bed. Feeling brazen and free, she climbed onto him and nibbled his ear.

"Holy hell," he whispered.

Chapter Twelve

Cynthia woke up alone in Declan's bed. Like his living room, the room was all male. It even smelled like him. The sun shone through a crack in the curtains. She checked her Fitbit, nine in the morning. She couldn't remember the last time she'd slept this late. She stretched like a cat enjoying the unusual feel of muscles strained by last night's exertions. Her cheeks bunched with an enormous smile. Even her heart was smiling.

Where was Declan? His pillow was cold; he'd been up for a while.

She could smell coffee. She'd kill for coffee right now. Maybe even with peppermint cream in it...in honor of the season. It was the middle of December. She'd have to get her shopping done soon. But first, Declan, and maybe a repeat performance of last night.

Jumping up from bed, she borrowed his toothbrush and hairbrush before slipping into her undergarments and a bathrobe she found on the back of the bedroom door.

Quietly, she crept downstairs and managed to find the kitchen. The house was enormous. Living room, television room, kitchen with eating area, empty formal dining room, laundry room, library, and one closed door.

Certain Declan was inside, she eased the door open and peeked her head around the corner. Yup. He was sitting in the near dark, his face a mask of concentration as he typed on his laptop. His fingers moved almost faster than she could comprehend. He must be on a roll. She sure wasn't going to break his concentration.

She returned to the kitchen for coffee. There was an empty mug on the counter. She sniffed it. Cream and sugar. It could belong to his brothers, but since nobody else seemed to be awake, she was going to assume it was Declan's. She found two clean mugs, prepped fresh cups, and carried his to the office. She crept in and set it on the coaster on his desk then turned to leave.

"Where are you going?" he growled. "Get back here. Give me a kiss."

"Sorry, I didn't mean to disturb you." She kissed his cheek.

He pulled her into his arms. "You aren't disturbing me; you inspire me, and that kiss isn't going to cut it. I need a real kiss for sustenance."

"One sec." She hurried to the door and closed it. Back at his side, stepped into his embrace, facing him. With a wiggle, she straddled his lap like she had the night before and pressed her lips to his. Her heart soared at the contact. This was heaven on earth.

She gave him the briefest peck on the lips. "Like that?"

"Yeah, I like that." He nibbled the corner of her lips. "But I meant like this." He dove in, taking the kiss deeper. Soft then firm. Tender and rough. He nibbled her lips, tasted her tongue. Her heart thundered in her ears. She grew hotter and hotter. She slipped her arms out of the robe without breaking the kiss.

Declan grew hard under her; his erection pressing up through his sweat pants. "Jeez," he growled. "You're wearing entirely too many clothes," he complained. "Why did you get dressed?'

"You call this dressed." She struggled to pull his T-shirt over his head. She needed to feel his naked skin against hers.

"Let's go upstairs. I can write later."

"Here. Now," she panted when he cupped her breasts.

"Whatever you want." He brushed aside some papers on the desk and sat her down, peeling her panties off as he went. "Damn. What did I ever do to deserve you?"

♥♥♥

Declan straightened the robe around Cynthia's shoulders and brushed a kiss across the top of her head. "You're going to kill me."

"Ya, I hear that." She laughed. "Again?"

"Already?" He groaned and rolled his eyes. Just thinking about it had him rock hard with need. "I can't. Honest to God, after last night and that encore, I need sustenance. Fortunately, I smell food. Someone else must be up."

Her face turned pink. "Oh, no. What if they heard us?" She was adorable, and sweet, and sexy. He was falling for her, hard.

"They'll be nice. I promise. At least until you leave. Then I'll get the ribbing of a lifetime." He took her hand, so soft and small in his. "Let's go find food. We'll face whatever comes together."

His brothers were busy cooking bacon and eggs. "Morning," he greeted them. "You two are up early."

"Morning." Ross grinned. "Food's just about done."

"Is there coffee?" She'd brought Dec's out with her, but the coffee she'd poured had turned stone cold during their interlude.

"Yup."

Declan sat at the table, pulling her into the chair by his side. He wrapped his arm around her and leaned his head against hers. She felt so perfect in his arms. Why had he waited so long to talk to her? He snorted to himself. He never did work up the courage, unless you counted the whole fake bear persona. She'd done all the work in this new relationship. He owed her big time. He'd have to find a way to make it up to her.

"How'd you get him out of the office?" Tom asked. "He's been holed up in there typing fast and furious since Winterfest."

"I asked nicely," she said, nudging Dec in the ribs.

"About damn time you guys started talking to each other," Ross grumbled. "How can two people be so stubborn?"

"This discussion is over. Can we just eat in peace?" He turned toward Cynthia. Damn, she was beautiful with messed up hair and just kissed lips. His heart thumped with tranquility and excitement. "What do you want to do today?"

"Can I read your manuscript?" She grinned.

"No. No. And hell no. Nobody reads until it's finished. Just to make sure you understand, nobody. Not even you." Her laughter caught him off guard.

"Can't hurt to ask." She winked.

Maybe breakfast could wait.

"What do you want to do today?" he repeated.

"I can't play today. I really need to go to Whitefalls and get some shopping done. It's almost Christmas," she said.

Disappointment rocked him. He didn't know what he thought they should do, but he assumed it would be together. "Bummer."

"You could come along if you like? Maybe grab a late lunch?" She sounded hopeful.

"Why not? I got a lot of words down while you were lazing away in bed. Let's eat and go." As if by magic, two plates appeared on the table in front of them. He looked up and his brothers were carrying their plates out of the room. Who knew they weren't jerks all the time?

Chapter Thirteen

Whitefalls's boutique shops were hopping. With only days to go until Christmas, there was only one shopping Saturday after today. People were rushing and bustling about, some frantic to get their gifts bought. The entire atmosphere was exhilarating for Cynthia, especially since she was strolling hand in hand with Declan.

"Wow, I wasn't expecting this," Declan said.

"Come on, Saturday, this close to Christmas? It would be weird if it wasn't nuts. Relax. Enjoy the feeling. I love the holidays. Christmas is my favorite time of year. The hustle, the bustle. People being extra nice and friendly. The decorations. I love the glitz and glitter. Well, not actual glitter, you can never clean that stuff up." She laughed.

"Let's approach this logically. Who do you need to buy for? Where should we shop first? Let's go."

"Whoa there, Mr. Famous Writer in a Rush. This is about the fun of the day. Enjoying the moments. Let's stroll, drink some cocoa. Eat mini donuts. Then, after some window shopping, we'll dive in. One cannot rush holiday shopping; you know that, right?" He had to be kidding.

"Um, actually, I usually shop online and have it delivered. Wrapped."

She gasped and feigned outrage. "Tell me you're joking."

"Not remotely. I have four gifts to buy this year. Five if I count you, and you won't be around for that. They're already ordered, except you. Today is about what you need, so lead on. Show me how it's done."

"Today, you learn a thing or two. Starting here and now." She stopped in front of a street vendor selling mini donuts and hot drinks. She ordered, and they fought a bit over who was going to pay. In the end, she let him buy, only to shut him up so they could get back to the happy business of shopping.

They walked up and down the busy street, peering into windows, smiling at other shoppers, chatting to each other. She was in heaven. She found the perfect earrings for Nora and a lovely scarf for Eve. They never spent much on each other, just enough to show they cared. Nora's daughter got a gift certificate to her favorite store. As a teen, she was impossible to shop for. She grabbed some boutique chocolates for each member of her staff. The town officials might not appreciate them enough for gifts, but she certainly did.

Declan followed along, carrying her bags and making ridiculous suggestions. She couldn't remember the last time she'd laughed so much. With everything purchased, except his gift, she was ready to eat.

"Why don't I meet you at the restaurant. I just have one thing left to pick up. I'll be ten minutes, tops."

"Sure. I'll go on ahead." His smile stretched from ear to ear.

Her heart swelled at his eagerness to make her happy. Everything he did made her happy. Sooner or later, she was going to convince him to let her read that manuscript. She giggled. That would never happen. She raised up on her toes and kissed him long enough that the people around them cheered when they broke apart. Declan bowed and strolled away, leaving her and their audience laughing.

She doubled back down the street to the toy store and popped inside. She grabbed what she needed and had it wrapped so he couldn't peek. She had a hunch that he'd be a peeker. The quiet ones always were.

He wasn't at the restaurant when she arrived, but he showed up breathless at their table only minutes later. "Sorry, I got sidetracked." He slid into the booth beside her and pressed a kiss on her cheek.

She was tickled that he sat beside her, but a little embarrassed at the same time. She finally decided to enjoy the moment and said to hell with what everyone else thought.

Lunch was delicious. The conversation even better, and the company divine.

"Have you noticed that since we actually managed to squeeze out the first words to each other, we never shut up?" she asked.

"That I have. It's weird. Good weird. I'm comfortable around you. I feel like I've known you all my life."

She couldn't stop her smile. "Ya, me too. I like you, Declan Foxx. I like you a lot. You really should have asked me out sooner."

"Yes, I should have."

♥♥♥

After texting her friends that she'd be out for another night, they returned to Declan's house for the evening. All through dinner, he was distracted, barely focusing on her or on his food.

"Enough," she declared. "Go. Write."

"I don't need to write," he said, though he still seemed distracted.

"Yes, you do. I've seen that look from both Eve and Nora. Your muse is calling, and you'll be totally useless to me until you satisfy her." She ran her fingers through his hair, admiring the gray flecks. "Don't worry about me. I'll borrow a book from you and read by the fireplace."

"Are you serious? Mom used to get upset when Dad spent extra hours at their sporting goods store."

"It used to bother me when the girls abandoned me. But I've learned that the muse can be fickle. Go. Now, while she's talking to you. I'll be here when you're done." She smiled into his serious brown eyes until they lightened in relief.

"You're the best." He jumped up from the table.

"Remember that next time I ask for a sneak peek." She made a shooing motion with her hands. "Be gone, DR Thomas. Be gone." She giggled when he saluted and raced away.

The man was something else. She leaned back in her chair, sipping the wine he'd poured her moments before. Contentment and love stole over her. It was totally crazy that she loved him already. It had only been days since she danced with him at Winterfest. Now, her heart was totally tangled in his, and she was pretty certain he felt the same.

Chapter Fourteen

Declan yawned as he climbed the stairs three nights later. He'd spent every day hard at work on his novel. He was more productive than he'd been in years. He had actually managed to scratch out a rough draft. Now, he had to read it and find the gaping plot holes. He clutched the printed manuscript in his hands. Thank heaven for recycling or he'd be killing the planet. Hard as he tried, he couldn't edit properly on screen; he needed paper.

Cynthia was already asleep in his bed. Their bed. She stayed with him every night, though often she was asleep before he shut down the computer. She was patient and understanding of being ignored. He appreciated it but had no idea how to show his gratitude.

She'd left the light burning on his nightstand. He undressed and climbed into bed beside her. Propped up against the headboard, he started to read. He tried to focus, but his legs ached. He shifted and tried again. His back wasn't right so he fluffed the pillows. After the fourth shift, he realized the problem wasn't his position, it was the silence. He always read the pages aloud, correcting as he went.

"What's wrong?" she asked sleepily, kissing his arm.

"I can't focus." It was so frustrating. If she wasn't here, there wouldn't be an issue. The trouble was that he wanted her beside him. He liked sleeping with her.

"Overtired?" She wiggled upward in bed and noticed the manuscript. "Oh, are you editing? Can I read it?"

She was teasing, he knew it. Suddenly, having her read the manuscript didn't seem like such a bad idea. "Usually, I read it aloud to myself, making changes as I go. Would you mind if I did that?"

She bolted upright. "Mind? Heck no." She made a hurry up gesture and grinned. "Get started."

He skipped over the dedication and acknowledgements, and the brief preamble that explained the previous books, and got straight to the story. "An explosion rocked Pippa in her bed. 'Warning. Warning. Hull breach.' The alarm screamed. In a fluid motion impossible under full gravity, Pippa rolled to her feet and shove-floated herself out of her cabin towards the control deck."

He stopped and made a correction with a red pen and started reading again.

Twice during the first chapter, Cynthia interrupted him with observations on changes that would improve the story. Both times, she was right. They worked on through the night. By morning, they were only halfway through. He set the manuscript aside.

"I have to sleep. My eyes feel like they're bleeding." He yawned.

"Me too. I'm calling in sick." She paused. "I've never done that. I always work unless I really am sick. But there's no way I can function today. I have to sleep." She texted someone and lay down facing him. She patted the bed. "Ditch the book. Come lay with me; I'll rub your back."

The generosity of the offer touched him. He leaned in and kissed her before placing the manuscript on the floor and lying beside her. She massaged his neck and shoulders. Just as he started drifting off, she whispered, "I love you." He was going to say it back, but exhaustion overcame him first.

They spent the next few nights reading and editing. During the daytime, he played with plot ideas for his next book. His muse was pushing ideas at him faster than he could write. It was exhilarating.

December twenty-first, the morning after they stayed up late decorating the Christmas tree and putting gifts under it, Declan woke to the shrill ringing of his cell phone. He looked at it. His publisher. "Morning, Dagan. How are you?"

"Mad as hell," Dagan yelled, his voice booming through the speaker.

"What? Why?"

"Because my ass is on the line, you idiot. The Sunday Times printed an excerpt of chapter one of your book. You know your contract. Nobody but your agent, you, and I see that manuscript before it goes to line edits. What the hell are you doing?"

Cynthia sat up and stared at him.

"I only sent it to my agent. She was supposed to forward it to you. I sure didn't send it out to anyone else. I'm not stupid." Hot anger raced up his spine. "Why the hell would my agent leak my novel?" It didn't make sense. Nobody else had access to it.

Except Cynthia.

He stared at her, questions and doubt in his expression.

She shook her head.

"I'll call you back." He hung up on Dagan.

"You can't think I'd do that," Cynthia backed away from him until she was perched on the edge of the bed, "I would never betray you like that."

"Somebody leaked it to the press, and you're the only other person with access. How could you?" He jumped out of bed and grabbed his sweats, pulling them over his naked backside. "I can't believe I trusted you."

She jumped up and started pulling on her clothes. Tears ran down her face. "I've never betrayed you in any way. Sure, this relationship is new, and I'm a huge fan, but I would never reveal your work to anyone. I love you too much for that. I'd never hurt you that way." She stumbled around, grabbing her clothing. Her sweater went on backwards, and it took two tries to get her pants on right. She paused, underwear and bra clutched in her hands, tears streaming down her face. "If you think I'd betray you that way, you're not the man I thought you were." Her chest heaved in anger. "I'm leaving now. I'll send you my schedule. Don't come into the library when I'm working or I'll have you arrested for harassment."

The urgent horror of knowing he'd screwed up slammed into him, stealing his breath and making him nauseous. "Cynthia, wait!"

The front door slammed as he thundered down the stairs after her. How had he been so stupid? She never would have done something like that, not even if she were mad at him. He raced outside, but she was already gone from sight.

He went back to his room to get dressed so he could follow her. He had to tell he that he'd messed up. He needed her. He loved her.

Chapter Fifteen

Cynthia hid in her room. It was a good thing the library was closed for the holiday season. Eve stuck her head into the room.

"I let you sleep all day yesterday. It's time to get up. You can't possibly be that heartbroken over a jerk like that. You've only known him a couple weeks," Eve said.

"I've known him for years!" Stupid point to make. "He actually accused me of leaking the first chapter of his manuscript to the press. It's insane. How could he think I'd do something like that?" He was such a jerk. She'd given him her heart, and she was sure she'd heard him whisper his love once.

She wasn't a child. She knew herself, and her emotions, but obviously, Declan didn't or he'd have never said such hurtful things to her.

"Come on. Get up. We'll have a bitch session about men downstairs. We'll drink wine and eat ice cream." Eve came over and hugged Cynthia. "It'll help, I promise. Plus, I can tell you about his jackass brother."

"What? What did he do to you?"

"Suffice it to say that Thomas Foxx is as big a jerk as his brother. They probably all are."

"This I have to hear." She wiped away her tears, blew her nose, and got up. She didn't feel up to it, but she washed her face and brushed her teeth before pulling on yoga pants. She stared at her bed, grateful that she'd never had Declan stay over. He'd never set foot in her room. At least she didn't have to burn her mattress.

Downstairs, she joined her friends in the living room, where Bing Crosby crooned about coming home and Christmas. Three pints of ice cream, a pot of coffee, and a large Hawaiian pizza sat on the coffee table. All her favorites. Too bad she wasn't hungry. "I thought there was going to be wine."

"I put Kahlua and peppermint schnapps in the coffee," Nora said. "Sit. Get comfortable and spill your guts."

She sat between her friends on the coach, overwhelmed with gratitude for their support and caring. Slowly, between sips of loaded coffee and bites of food, she spilled the story. He'd been so kind and romantic after they'd finally connected. Then, in a heartbeat, he'd turned on her for something she hadn't done.

"Want me to slash his tires?" Eve asked.

Cynthia laughed. "You're the most Zen person I ever met. You're practically a peacenik. I can't see you slashing tires." The laughter felt good. Maybe she could get over him.

"For you, I'd break my Zen and go all wildcat on him."

The doorbell rang.

They looked at each other. "I'm not here," she declared, crossing her arms over her chest. "He can go just go away."

Nora went to the door and came back with a package addressed to Cynthia. "It's heavy and it's from a bookstore in Calgary. What did you order?"

"Nothing. Let me see." The thought of new books almost cheered her up. The distraction would be nice. She tore into the package. It contained six first editions books. Nothing super old, but two of them were autographed by the author. "Holy cow. These are worth a mint. I didn't order them."

Eve dug through the wrapping. "Here's a note. It's typed." She read it to herself before passing it over. It was printed on a one-sided Christmas card with a jolly Santa and snowman on the front.

I'm a jackass. Forgive me? Dec

"Well at least he knows he messed up, unlike his brother," Eve declared.

"What about his brother?" Cynthia asked. "What did he do?"

"I don't want to talk about it. Suffice it to say he won't be coming over anymore."

"That can't be good." Cynthia should have been more sympathetic, but her own woes were dragging her down. He'd been such a jerk and now this. The perfect gift. The apology sucked, because it wasn't one, it was just an admission of guilt. But the gift was incredible.

The doorbell rang again. "Still not home," she said.

Eve brought in an enormous bouquet of poinsettias and a box of truffles. Another card, this only simply signed, Love, Declan. They ate the truffles and griped about men, while she tried her best to ignore the flowers and the gesture they held.

The next delivery was a knit scarf and hat, both patterned with books. That was followed by a dress in exactly her size. It too was printed in books, and it had pockets. A tray of desserts from the bakery and peppermint hot chocolate for the trio of women arrived. The man had a knack for gifts, but his attempts to win her back were useless. He hadn't trusted her; he didn't deserve her. When the bell rang again, she was sure it would be another delivery.

For the first time, she got off the couch and went to the door. She yanked it open.

Declan. *Crap. Just what she didn't need.* He held a brightly wrapped parcel in his hands, as if another gift would sway her heart. A thousand gifts weren't enough. She wasn't impressed with material things. She needed…more.

"What are you doing here?" she demanded. She hated the warble in her voice that revealed her turbulent emotions. "You can go." Preferably before she caved and threw herself into his arms.

"Can I come in?" He strode past her, just as she had passed him the night she invaded his home. He hung up his jacket and kicked off his boots and headed for the living room. "Ladies, can we have some privacy? I have some groveling to do."

"No," Nora said.

"Yes," Eve dragged Nora from the room leaving them alone; the gaping silence vibrated around them. Every nerve ending was attuned to him, reaching for him. Needing him. Her skin, her mind, her heart, and her soul cried out for him.

He walked across the room and stood in front of the Christmas tree, and she was reminded that he'd felt like a gift from the gods to her lonely heart. She wanted to run to him, to forgive his mistake, but every part of her was wary and ached with betrayal. Of all the things one person could do to another, being betrayed by someone you loved and trusted was the worst and the hardest to recover from.

She breathed deeply, trying to still the frantic beat of her heart and thrum of her pulse. Being in his arms, sharing his world had been perfect; a dream come true that turned into a nightmare. She crossed her arms over her chest and backed as far from him as the room allowed. If she were close, she'd touch him, and then she'd be lost.

She wasn't going to open this conversation. He could speak first. He'd said he was here to grovel. Let him beg for all she cared. She was done. She was too old for his bull crap.

He looked tired. She couldn't believe they'd made sweet love less than two weeks ago. Afterward, she'd watched him, his face relaxed in sleep, a small smile on his lips. Despite the gray sprinkled through his hair, he'd looked young. Today, he'd aged twenty years. He looked haggard. She'd done that to him.

No! He'd done that to himself!

The silence dragged on for two minutes, then four. He swallowed hard, his Adam's apple bobbing repeatedly. He stuffed his hands into his pockets and pulled them out again. He looked everywhere, except at her. He was nervous. Good; he deserved to be uncomfortable.

"Look, Cyn." He cleared his throat. "I messed up. There's no excuse for what I said, for what I did. I am so sorry." He strode toward her and thrust the heavy package into her arms before backing away.

"Finally, he gets something right." She couldn't stop the snarky remark, but managed to clamp her mouth shut before she said anything else.

"You came into my life like a quiet tornado. You mixed up the world the first time I noticed you. You woke feelings in me I had no idea I was capable of." His hands went back into his pockets.

Okay, that wasn't bad.

"I've had a weird life. I was the geeky kid that girls ignored. I was nervous and shy and couldn't talk to girls. Not at all. I thought all that changed the week before prom when Francine Boatman asked me to take her to the dance. God, I was ecstatic. She was beautiful. Head cheerleader, most popular girl in the school, and she wanted to go out with me. Me! I couldn't believe it. I shouldn't have believed it. One day she wouldn't even acknowledge my existence, the next she asked me out." He gave a sarcastic laugh. "It was too good to be true, and I took it at face value. I was a naïve idiot. She dumped me at the door to the gym. Publicly. Told me she'd only done it to win a bet with her friends. She bet them a hundred bucks each that she'd do it. She needed the money to fix her car."

Her heart hurt from the pain he'd endured.

He shook his head. "She left me standing there, in the gym doorway, half of our graduating class laughing, the other half looking embarrassed for me. She laughed and walked away, arm in arm with the captain of the football team. I was devastated. The stupid thing was, aside from her being a mean girl, I had the skills and would have fixed her car for free if she had asked."

"Holy...the witch." What heartbreak that must have been to a youth on the cusp of adulthood.

"It broke something in me. Before I gathered my wits enough to leave, one of the other girls asked me to dance. I snapped and told her I didn't want a pity dance. I got the hell out of there as fast as my legs would carry me." His voice trembled with remembered emotion. She saw the pain gouging his heart, and her own heart wept for his hurts.

"That was the day my shyness took over. Don't get me wrong, I was never good at talking to girls. That day shut me down. Completely. I probably should have gotten help. Instead, I lived with it. Over time, I learned I could talk to older women, or women who were obviously in relationships. You know, married or toting children around. But beautiful women who might be single, like you? Not a chance. My mouth goes dry, and I can't form a coherent thought. I spent my entire life that way. It bothered me, but not enough to do anything about it. I probably should have talked to a professional about it."

His eyes pleaded for understanding. She longed to rush to his side, to embrace him and kiss away all his past hurts. Nobody deserved to live like that, least of all a wonderful man like Declan.

"Then you came along. So beautiful, so kind. You have no idea how much it hurt me not to talk to you. My muse dried up. My failure to approach you dug deep into my psyche. I stopped writing. I couldn't write. You want to know why it's been so long since the last book? It's not because of supply chain issues, or publishing problems, it's because my stupid, stubborn mind wouldn't write because I was a failure."

"You are not a failure." How could she be the cause of his writer's block? It crushed her heart. She trembled with need to go to him, but she sensed he wasn't finished. She tried to look reassuring.

"Then, one day, you spoke to me. You asked me how my day was. That day, I got a few words down. But the ideas just wouldn't come. Every time I saw you, it became more difficult to talk to you. I didn't see that you found it hard to talk to me too. I watched you talk to other patrons. Long conversations about books and life. I didn't understand why you didn't do the same with me. You have no idea how much I wanted to talk to you."

"I wanted to talk to you too. I'm not an outgoing person. I'm not an introvert either. I can talk to people. But with you, I could never get more than a few sentences past the lump in my throat and the trembling in my knees. Not until I realized who you were. Knowing you were DR Thomas released something in me."

"Best day of my life." His smile was sad. "Anyway. I had my agent calling me three times a week looking for the next installment, even a few chapters would have satisfied her. My editor was even worse. Daily calls and emails. I sunk into my failure. It was like quicksand. The longer I was bogged down, the harder it got to break free. Then, the papers started questioning if there was ever going to be a new book. One even speculated that I had died. Turns out that my desire to be anonymous played into that. If I'd been open, maybe done some interviews, the rumors wouldn't have started." He laughed wryly and puffed out a breath.

She could see his pain and embarrassment in his stiff shoulders and restless hands. "I'm sorry for what you went through. But that's no excuse for how you treated me. I loved you, and you turned on me for something I'd never do." She hated him for that.

She wanted to run at him and pound on his chest until he realized how deep he'd sliced into her heart. She should tell him to leave, before she caved and took him back. She deserved better than a man who didn't trust her.

"Then, I got that call. The one saying the opening pages of my manuscript were in the newspaper. Nobody had seen it except you, my agent, and my publisher. My publisher, Dagan, was off the wall pissed. I freaked and lashed out at you. That was a colossal mistake. I know you'd never do anything like that. Never."

"And yet you blamed me. Don't you know how honored I was to be part of your creative process? To help you perfect the story? It was a dream come true for me. I'd never loved a man the way I loved you. You became part of me and then you destroyed me." She'd cried until there were no tears left and then cried without them. She'd raged and pouted and screamed until she had no voice. His betrayal had cut to the bone and ripped out her heart.

Was that how he'd felt? Had what he thought was her betrayal destroyed him?

"I've never loved anyone the way I love you." He took a step toward her and stopped when she raised her hand as if to block his advance. "I couldn't believe you'd do that to me. I know you didn't betray me. I jumped to conclusions. I thought this was just another cheap shot by a beautiful woman. It was high school all over again. You were so kind to me and such a fan of my work. For a heartbeat, I thought you used me for your own gain. That you'd sold the story for profit."

"What? How could you think that of me?" Any softening toward him she might have been feeling fled with his words. She was right; he was a total jerk and unworthy of her.

He paced in front of the beautifully lit Christmas tree, the joyful lights making a mockery of her broken heart.

"Funny thing was, I didn't believe it. Even as I said the words, I knew you'd never do that to me. You aren't like Francine. You're kind and generous and loving. I overreacted to an imagined slight because I'm too stubborn to get over something a petty, greedy teenage girl did to me over thirty years ago. I came here to apologize. Cynthia, I was an ass, and I apologize for doubting you. Please come back to me." His voice trembled and his fists clenched at his sides like he was holding himself in check; forcing himself to stay still and not rush to her side.

She was tempted. Everyone made mistakes, right? He'd slashed her heart out of her chest and stomped on it. What would stop him from doing that again?

"And the next time your words are leaked? Will you blame me again? Will you throw me out of your house and out of your life?" She had to know how he felt.

"Jeez. No! I know you. I know you'd never do that to me. I messed up. I can't take those accusations back, but every part of me wishes I could. I love you, Cynthia Jones, my beautiful librarian. I'd give up writing for you. I'll give you everything if you'll just take me back."

The ice around her heart cracked at the sincerity of his voice, but she couldn't make herself thaw. She stared at him, dry eyed, her limbs trembling with need to go to him. It took everything she had not to rush to his side.

"How did the story leak?" It was one of the many questions he'd yet to answer, and she needed to know because it sure wasn't her who went to the press.

"When my publisher, Dagan, heard that I was halfway through the book, he put it up for preorder and put out a press release that it was coming soon. There were a few orders, not many. Readers can be fickle and after a long hiatus, rather unforgiving.

"My agent—sorry, my ex-agent—took matters into her own hands. She decided that if people were able to read a rough excerpt, they'd flock to stores and order the book. She put it out there. She wanted the money I used to generate for her. She betrayed me, and I fired her." He stepped toward her, a hopeful expression on his face.

She shook her head. She didn't want him any closer.

He dropped to his knees and clasped his hands together like he was praying. "I've made a decision. No matter what happens between us. That story is yours, and yours alone. It will never be published. It's my gift to you. DR Thomas's gift to the only fan that matters. *End Space* will never see another set of eyes except yours. I'll break my contract and leave the series hanging. Forever."

What was he thinking? The world needed those words. They needed the entertainment, and the small messages of hope and joy that all his books gave readers. Those messages were part of the reason she was addicted to his stories. Give up his future contracts and royalties for her? The idea was ridiculous. "You'd lose thousands of dollars."

"Probably hundreds of thousands," he corrected. "But I don't care; money is nothing. Words are nothing. Not unless I have you at my side, in my life, in my heart. Whatever you want, I'll give it to you. Nothing matters except you and your happiness." He stayed there, on his knees, looking up at her, his aching heart reflected in his eyes.

"You're not serious." He couldn't be. Nobody would give up their passion for another person. The idea was ludicrous.

"I am serious. Read this." He pulled out his phone and scrolled before handing it to her. "Tanis is my editor. Read the texts."

She set the parcel on the table, took the phone, and stared into his eyes. She saw the sincerity there. He had such expressive eyes; they stole her breath. She glanced down at the phone, intending to give it a cursory glance. She read one line, then another. Unable to believe what she was reading, she scrolled further back. The entire text stream was his editor begging him not to pull the story. Then threatening him with legal action if he did. The final two texts convinced her.

Tanis: No woman is worth giving up your passion and career for. You'll regret this. You'll never have another contract. I'll bury your ass. Nobody in the publishing world will ever read another one of your manuscripts.

Declan: I don't care. She's worth it. I'd give up everything I have for her happiness. The story is hers and hers alone. Consider our contract ended. You stole my work. You are fired.

"You did it. You actually cut your contract? Are you insane?" She stared at him. Disbelief. "Why would you do that? It'll cost you a fortune in lost revenue and legal fees." Part of her was astounded that he'd done something so crazy. The rest was touched by the gesture.

"Why? Haven't you been listening? Because nothing in the world, not money, not fame, nothing is more important to me than you. I'd give up writing for you. I'd give up my life for you, Cynthia. I might not know much about life and love, but I do know two things for certain. One, I'm a colossal idiot for jumping to conclusions, and two, my life is worth nothing if you aren't in it. I'm begging you to take me back. Please. I'm literally on my knees here."

He stood and grabbed the parcel from the table and held it toward her. "Open it. Please."

She debated refusing. She should refuse. She should walk away and end this, but her heart screamed for her to stay, to forgive him. Everyone made mistakes? Didn't they?

She took the package. "Oof. It's heavy."

"That's the weight of my heart."

For a writer, he had the corniest lines. She almost smiled. She sat on the couch with the package on her lap. Slowly, she picked at the tape holding it shut. Declan paced, like he wanted to holler at her to hurry up. She folded each piece of tape and set it on the table. She looked up at him and was nearly floored by the hope and desperation in his chocolate eyes. He raked a hand through his hair. The brown strands settled, but the gray stayed upright. He looked demented, and too damned adorable.

She peeled the paper away to reveal a plain white box. She realized it was the exact size of a sheet of printer paper. She sucked in a breath. Without opening the box, she knew it was the manuscript. He was doubling down on his promise to give it to her.

"Open it," he pleaded.

She lifted off the lid. The box held the manuscript, complete with the edits they'd worked on together. There was also a thumb drive. "What's this?" She held up the drive.

"That's the only digital copy. I've erased it from my drive, my backup drive, and my backup-backup drive. You now possess the only copies. Print and electronic.

Both my ex-agent and my publisher have destroyed their copies. I know, because I flew there and did it myself. That's why I'm so late coming to you."

He was serious. Heart touchingly serious. She couldn't resist that. She lifted the top sheet and came face to face with the dedication page.

For Cynthia. Owner of my heart, keeper of my dreams, and inspiration for my words. I love you beyond life itself.

She blinked back tears and tossed the manuscript aside. She jumped into his arms. He wobbled precariously back and forth. "I love you." She rained kisses all over his face. She brushed her lips over his. Her tongue stole inside to caress his. She wiggled, desperate to get closer to fuse their bodies together. She kissed him there, in the glow of the Christmas tree, before the crackling fire. She was finally home.

"I love you," he murmured against her mouth. "I'm so sorry. If I'm ever being a jackass again, tell me, for the love of Christmas and all that's holy, tell me. Before I drive you away."

"You can bet your Christmas tree on that."

"Just one more thing." He dropped to his knees and pulled a black velvet box from his pocket. He flipped it open to reveal a small heart shaped diamond, with a tiny green stone on either side. "You're the diamond in my life, and the emeralds match your eyes. You leave me breathless. Will you marry me?"

She dropped to her knees beside him. "Absolutely."

"Best Christmas ever." He leaned in and claimed her mouth with love and passion like she'd never known before.

"It sure is. I love you, Declan Foxx, with all my heart."

"I love you too, Cynthia Jones."

If you enjoyed this story, please check out the other books in this series or my other Christmas books.
A Melody for Christmas
Coming Home for Christmas
Sleigh Bells Inn
Christmas in Silver Creek.

About Katie O'Connor

Best-selling author Katie O'Connor lives in Calgary, Alberta, Canada. She married her high school sweetheart and is living her happily ever after. She is the mother of two grown daughters and is extremely proud of her five grandchildren.

She is the founder of The Write Chicks, a private romance writers' group set up with the sole purpose of supporting each other's writing career. She belongs to several other writing organizations.

Katie's career path has been long and twisted, with most of her life devoted to her family. She's been a waitress, chambermaid, cashier, store manager, as well as a lab and X-ray technician. She's been a small business owner and is an avid quilter and crafter.

She's dabbled in writing since high school because something drives her to create stories. She swears it's impossible for her NOT to write. Unsatisfied with one genre, Katie writes contemporary romance, erotic romance, fantasy/paranormal romance, romantic suspense, and erotica.

Katie believes in all things magical, including dragons, fairies, UFOs, ghosts, and house pixies. But most of all she believes in love, romance, and hope.

Where to Find Katie

One of Katie's favorite things is hearing from her readers. If you enjoyed this book, don't hesitate to reach out and let Katie knows.

Email: katie@katieohwrites.com
Newsletter Signup: http://eepurl.com/Q2nRr
Website: https://katieohwrites.com
Facebook: http://www.facebook.com/katieohwrites

Katie O'Connor

Katie's Books

<u>Contemporary Romance by Katie</u>

<u>Heart's Haven</u>
Running Home
Saving Grace
Building Trust

<u>Coyote Creek</u>
A Lesson in Love
A Heart Torn Apart
A Secret to Shatter
A Melody for Christmas
A Surrender so Sweet
A Place Called Home
A Love to Rebuild
Coming Home for Christmas

<u>A Silver Fox Christmas</u>
Their Perfect Christmas
Their Christmas Heart
Their Christmas Love

Their Christmas Heart

Contemporary Romance Single Title
To a Tea
Rekindled Fire
Hearts in the Spotlight (A Women of Stampede Novel)
Cupid's Charm
Gingerbread Dreams
Christmas in Silver Creek
Sleigh Bells Inn (A Christmas at the Inn Novella) (Dec. 2022)

Romantic Suspense
Protecting Josie
Bulletproof Heart

Paranormal Romance
Fire Magic (Three Moon Falls Book One)
Water Magic (Three Moon Falls Book Two)

Career Planning
Creative Career Planning Workbook for Authors

Erotic Romance/Erotica

Stand Alone Erotic Romances
Tessa's Trio
The Gift
Covet the Cowboy Erotic Romance Series
Corralling the Cowboy (Book 1)
Cornering the Cowgirl (Book 2)

www.ingramcontent.com/pod-product-compliance
Lightning Source LLC
Chambersburg PA
CBHW051542050726
47595CB00002B/598